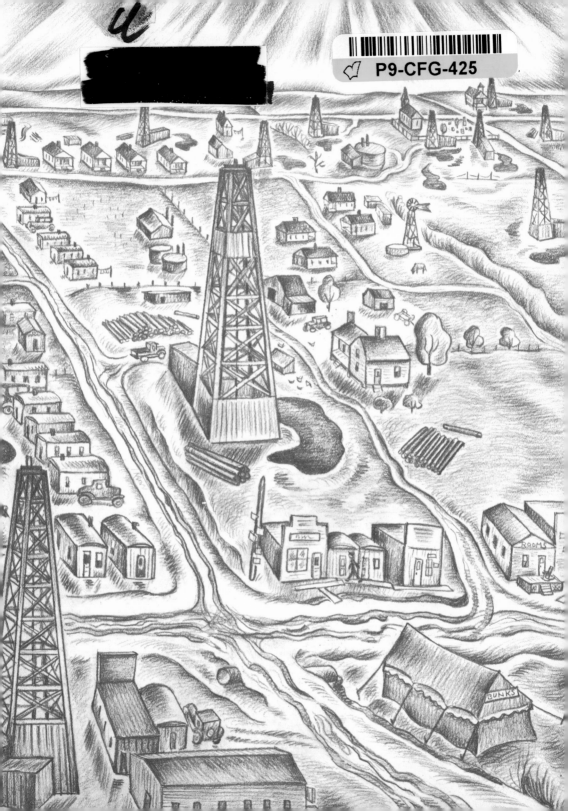

Boom Town Boy

Other Books by Lois Lenski

Autobiographical

A LITTLE GIRL OF NINETEEN HUNDRED

Historical

PHEBE FAIRCHILD, HER BOOK
A-GOING TO THE WESTWARD
BOUND GIRL OF COBBLE HILL
OCEAN-BORN MARY
INDIAN CAPTIVE
BLUEBERRY CORNERS
PURITAN ADVENTURE

Regional

BAYOU SUZETTE
STRAWBERRY GIRL
BLUE RIDGE BILLY
JUDY'S JOURNEY
BOOM TOWN BOY
COTTON IN MY SACK
TEXAS TOMBOY
PRAIRIE SCHOOL
MAMA HATTIE'S GIRL
CORN FARM BOY
SAN FRANCISCO BOY
FLOOD FRIDAY
HOUSEBOAT GIRL
COAL CAMP GIRL

For my
Oklahoma
Nieces and Nephews

BOOM TOWN BOY

Written & Illustrated

by

LOIS LENSKI

1948

J. B. Lippincott Company
New York & Philadelphia

PRINTED IN THE UNITED STATES OF AMERICA

Ninth Printing

Library of Congress catalog card number 48-2379

CONTENTS

KANSAS

CHEROKEE STRIP

Settled Sept. 16, 1893

TONKAWA

WHIZZBANG

ENID

PONCA CITY

1
2
3

PERRY

OSAGE NATION

PAWHUSKA

BARTLESVILLE

CHEROKEE NATION

TULSA

Mo

Texas

"OLD OKLAHOMA"

Settled
April 22, 1889

GUTHRIE

OKLAHOMA CITY

CREEK NATION

SEMINOLE

OTHER TRIBES

CHICKASAW NATION

INDIAN TERRITORY

CHOCTAW NATION

INDIAN RESERVATIONS
1 TONKAWAS
2 PONCAS
3 OTOES

T E X A S

N

W   E

S

Picture Map
of
OKLAHOMA

Foreword

The amazing thing about Oklahoma is its oldness and its newness—the oldness of its Indian civilization, and the newness of its white settlement. In a man's lifetime, it has passed from the pioneer stage to modern civilization. There are men and women living today who settled in Old Oklahoma at its opening in 1889—only fifty-eight years ago; and others who made the Run in the opening of the Cherokee Strip in 1893—fifty-four years ago. Children who went in with their parents and lived in sod houses are now in their sixties and early seventies, and remember their experiences vividly.

These land openings were phenomenal. Towns were built overnight. Like swarms of locusts, the people came, took claims and settled on the land. Many people have felt that nothing like it could ever happen again, but it could and did. Where? In Oklahoma.

The oil booms were equally phenomenal. Beginning in the early 1900's, and continuing for some thirty years, the early 1920's were the peak of the oil boom period. Again, towns were built overnight. Again like swarms of locusts, the people came and settled, this time not to get land, but money. The only thing in American history comparable to the oil boom was the gold rush in the Far West, where boom towns also sprang up, and where good and bad people swarmed, in the hope of getting rich quickly.

Oil booms took place in other states, too—in Pennsylvania, Louisiana, Texas, California, etc. But in Oklahoma, the drama of oil was heightened by contributory factors—by the recentness of its settlement, by the unproductiveness of the land and the struggle involved in getting a bare living.

Oil booms are now a thing of the past. They can never happen again. Oil wells are no longer allowed to run wild and devastate the country— the product is too valuable. The oil industry has profited by its early experiences and learned effective means of control and conservation, which are rigidly enforced.

The coming of oil in the boom period is a dramatic story, one of the most dramatic chapters in the history of our country. Fortunes were made in a day and lost as quickly. People were hurled from poverty to sudden riches. Those who did not know how to handle money promptly lost it through bad expenditures, investments or swindles, and went back to poverty again. Some few accomplished a great deal of good with their money. Those who lived through the experience of becoming suddenly rich, and salvaged from it a commendable way of life for themselves were fortunate. There is no question but that oil money, wisely used, benefited thousands of Oklahoma families and gave a chance in life to thousands of Oklahoma children who would never have had it otherwise.

There is so much American history still unwritten. I read a number of books on the subject of oil as a background for this story, but I could not find in them the information I needed. Only from the lips of living people can this kind of history be obtained. I went to Oklahoma to find out how it felt to live through an oil boom.

The rapid change from farm region to oil field must have been catastrophic to those who experienced it. I tried to get at it. I tried to get beneath the surface, and find out what it did to people. I talked to many people who had experienced oil in different ways.

I talked to children who grew up in oil fields; to girls who lived so sheltered they never suspected there was evil or wickedness in the neighborhood, or if they knew, lived in abject fear of it; to boys who, despite their mothers' fears and admonitions, did know what was going on about them. All the mothers insisted that they had carefully shielded their growing boys from the harsher side of oil field life, but the boys themselves told a different story.

For the past fifty years, through all the Oklahoma farmer's struggle to wrest a living from the land, he has carried a vision of the miracle of oil, which would come one day to release him from that struggle. I have talked to farm people, still full of eagerness and hope for the oil miracle to happen. Some men are bad farmers because they lean too heavily on this miracle—they dream too much of dreams that may never be realized.

I have seen in the face of a woman of seventy the fierce eagerness of that dream. She has seen oil money wreck people's lives, but it has not disturbed that dream. She has lived unselfishly for others all her life, but when she speaks of the possible coming of oil, her tired face beams with new life and her work-worn hands reach out greedily for easy money. She has worked so hard, she now covets money she did not earn. She lives in the hope that money may fall like manna from heaven into her lap. The amazing thing about this dream is its tenacity.

I talked to a devout man who said that God had revealed to him the presence of oil on his farm, who waited fifty years for the miracle to happen, and when it did, gave one hundred dollars from his first oil check to his church as a payment of gratitude.

I have talked to people who invested money—often their life-time savings—in oil, to lose or profit thereby. The strange thing is that so many of them, after years of up-and-down speculation, have come back to about the same level where they started.

I have talked to oil workers who knew oil's sordidness, its uncompromising demands in the way of long hours and heavy labor, and the thrill of its production. There is no question but that oil gets into men's blood. They sacrifice much for the thrill of adventure that it brings. They lived, and still live, unsettled, nomadic lives, carrying their families from one field to another because they love the work. They often come face to face with danger and death. I have talked to women who sacrificed husband or son to oil, and can speak of it now without bitterness. In the early boom days, the hazards were great and many men lost their lives. With modern methods of production has come greater safety.

I listened to many opinions about oil. To some it was a cruel monster who devoured people and wrecked lives. To others, it was a beneficent god, bringing riches, prosperity and happiness. In one part of Oklahoma, where oil is now being drilled, every one is greedy for the money that oil will bring. Only one man said: "I wonder if folks here will be any happier when they get oil and have all that money."

For every story of happiness and benefit caused by oil money, I heard a dozen stories of ruin and wreckage of people's lives—stories of family quarrels, of sons who dissipated and went to the bad, of daughters who made unwise marriages; of families who went through large fortunes in a hurry, and were left poorer than they had been at the start.

These are comments I heard:

"The more you get, the more you want."

"Money's not everything, but it helps."

"Oil money comes easy and goes easy."

"Rich one day and broke the next."

"Oil brings happiness—at least at first."

"Oil has ruined more people than crime or vice."

I did not hear any one repeat a statement made long ago which I thought of often as I listened: "The love of money is the root of all evil." One woman came near it when she said: "Material wealth does not bring happiness."

*   *   *

I have not attempted to portray a specific boom town, but have preferred to draw a composite picture, using incidents that happened in several localities. The general location is that formerly called "Three Sands." The name "Whizzbang" was actually the name of an oil town near Shidler, now a ghost town. My characters are imaginary, but most of the incidents used are taken from actual experience. I have made use of a few public figures of the period.

I have put less emphasis on the technical side of oil production, and none at all on its distribution or the advantages of oil to our civilization, as these aspects are usually covered in material generally available for school use. My emphasis has been on the human side, the drama of the coming of oil into a community—what it meant to one family, how it disturbed and disrupted their lives; what an upsetting thing sudden wealth can be, and how futile the pursuit of riches; and how the family is obliged to stop and think, to decide for themselves what constitutes happiness and how to use money as a constructive rather than a destructive force.

I am grateful to friends in Perry, Tonkawa, Ponca City, Shidler and Oklahoma City who helped me to understand their region and who shared with me their oil knowledge and experiences. In particular, I wish to thank Mr. Bert Woodruff, Miss Ruth Brookhart, Mrs. Ethel Konklin, also other members of my husband's family living in Perry and vicinity; Mrs. Ann Hough, Children's Librarian of Carnegie Library, and other friends in Oklahoma City, who gave me not only a graphic picture of the oil boom there, but a great deal of encouragement. I wish to thank Mr. Russell Hogin of the American Petroleum Institute and Mr. N. D. Drake of the Standard Oil Company for checking my manuscript for technical errors.

I have consulted Oklahoma: A Guide to the Sooner State; This Fascinating Oil Business *by Max W. Ball;* Flowing Gold *by John J. Floherty;* Then Came Oil *by C. B. Glasscock;* Oil Boom *by Boyce House; other volumes on general Oklahoma background; also newspaper and magazine articles.*

Lois Lenski

Perry, Oklahoma—Spring, 1947
Greenacres, Harwinton, Connecticut—Summer and Fall of 1947

CHAPTER I

On the Farm

"IT'S your turn, Addie."

"No-sir-ree, you only pumped ninety-eight strokes," retorted the small girl. "You stopped countin' at ninety-eight."

"Well, I'm awful tired," said Orvie. "You're younger and spryer'n I am. If you jump up and down while you pump, it makes it go faster. Golly, you're so little and quick, Addie, you'll get to one hundred in no time."

Little Addie, with freckled face, straw-colored windblown hair and plump arms and legs, took hold of the iron pump handle and pushed it vigorously up and down.

"One, two, three, four . . . five, six, seven, eight . . ." Orvie began counting for her.

"Pump handle's so hot, it's blisterin' my hands," complained

Addie. "It's too hard for me to pump . . ."

Ten-year-old Orvie slouched down on the dusty ground and leaned against the twelve-foot water tank.

"It takes a hundred and fifty strokes to raise the water one inch," he said lazily. "I measured it with my school ruler. When you pump an inch, I'll take my turn. Fifteen, sixteen, seventeen . . ." His voice went on counting as the girl's feet danced up and down.

It was late afternoon on a Sunday in September. The sun shone down fiercely on the dry Oklahoma pasture and flooded with its glare the two children under the windmill.

The pasture grasses were dry and dead. There were no trees except in the distance where the flat field suddenly dipped to a hollow. There, in a deep gully, a shallow creek made its way. There were no birds to sing in the heat. The shrill rasp of the katydid and the chirp of the cricket made it feel hotter than it really was.

"Thirty, thirty-one, thirty-two . . ." counted Orvie.

"Why's it got to be so still?" cried Addie. "Why we got to have so many still days anyhow? Why don't the wind never blow any more?"

"Wind don't never blow when the water tank's empty, you know that," said Orvie in a disgusted tone. He looked lazily up at the big wheel of the windmill overhead. He puffed his cheeks out and began to blow upward. "I'll start it for you, if I can get enough breath. Whew! Whew!"

But the big wheel did not turn.

"Fifty-six, fifty-seven, fifty-eight . . ." continued the boy.

"*Orvie!*" Addie screamed. "There's that old cow comin' again.

She drinks a tubful every time and we'll *never* get the tank full."

A cow came up to the tank. She sank her nose in the cool water and drank. Orvie and Addie picked up sticks and began to pummel her, but she kept on drinking.

Orvie dropped his stick. "It's no use—likely she's thirsty."

"Guess so," said Addie, dropping hers. Perspiration ran down her face, now red with the heat. She dropped to the ground and leaned against the tank. "You pump now, Orvie. Here come the horses."

Six horses came across the pasture and took drinks at the tank. Orvie picked up his stick and measured. "They've drunk three inches," he said in despair. "Three times a hundred and fifty . . . it'll take four hundred and fifty strokes to get it up to this wet water line, and it's six inches more to the top . . ." The arithmetic proved too much for him, so he just stood and watched the horses. "Likely they're thirsty," he said. "Cold water tastes best thing in the wide world on a hot day. Addie, I think . . ."

But Addie did not hear him.

"Where you goin'? You better come back here and help me pump, Addie."

Addie's feet were taking her swiftly across the pasture in the direction of Cottonwood creek. Orvie knew she was heading for the shade. She was going wading in the cool water. The boy's first impulse was to follow her. He looked up at the sky, hopeful of seeing a cloud which might bring a gust of wind. He looked at the windmill, wishing that by some magic the wheel might start turning and fill the tank in a few minutes.

But all was still. The air was filled with a deadly stillness. Nothing moved—it seemed as if nature had stopped breathing.

Orvie did not dare go away with his chore undone. He had been taught to obey, and he knew disobedience brought punishment. Addie was the littlest, "the pet" of the family—she could do as she pleased.

The horses kept on drinking. The old cow came back for another tubful. Orvie decided there was no use pumping until they had their fill. Suddenly an idea struck him and he put it into immediate action. He began to climb the ladder at the side of the tower. Now and then he looked down at the ground beneath him, but it did not make him dizzy. On and on, up and up he went until he reached the top. He drew a deep breath. He had never been clear to the top before.

It was a magnificent moment.

He looked all around and felt like a king. The farmhouse and barn looked smaller than they really were. He saw the pigs in their pen in the barnyard, and the chickens scratching and raising a dust. He saw Grandpa's small house, set in the yard under a cottonwood tree. He wondered how it felt to live all alone in a brooder house, and where Grandpa had gone this afternoon. His eye scanned the pasture and the field plowed for winter wheat beyond. It swept the horizon on all sides. If only the windmill were a little higher, he could see Texas to the south and west, Arkansas to the east and Kansas north. But all he could see were wide fields that had once been prairie, fenced into quarter-sections. The earth looked small, so wide and open was the sky.

Orvie thought of Addie again. He couldn't see her. She had disappeared in the bushes along the creek. He decided to follow her . . . He looked down. The cows and horses had wandered off in the field, and there below him, to his surprise, stood his father, all dressed up in his Sunday suit.

"Orvie! Orville Robinson!" came his father's voice. "What you doin' up there?"

All of a sudden the boy was scared. He hadn't realized how high the windmill was before. He clung to the metal framework and his face turned white. His father's face was a white mask below him. He could hear words coming out of his father's mouth, but could not make out what they were.

"Oh Lord, help me to get down and not be scared," he prayed in a whisper. His fear disappeared and his feet found the rungs of the ladder.

"If you can't climb down without falling," he heard his father say, "I'll sure blister you."

He made up his mind he would not fall, and he didn't. When he stood on his feet beside his father, he noticed that his father looked scared and was not cross at all.

"You should have pulled the wheel out of gear, Orvie. If the wind had started blowing, that wheel would have knocked you down," Papa said. "Get busy and pump the tank full. Where's Addie?"

"Gone to the creek," he said.

"Get your pumping done and go bring her home." Papa walked away.

The pumping went faster now. When the tank was nearly full, he scurried off over the prairie to the creek. The stream of water was down in a dirt gully, between steep embankments. The shade was cool and inviting.

Addie had taken off her shoes and stockings and was wading.

[5]

The Murray girls, Edna Belle and Nellie Jo, plain-faced and plump, stood on the high bank, dressed in Sunday dresses with white pinafore aprons. They wore shiny slippers and long white stockings, and were afraid to wet their feet. Downstream, Orvie saw two Indian children, Harry Big Bear and Lily Wild Berry, digging crawfish. They were the grandchildren of old White Cloud, whom he often saw at the country store.

Orvie ran over and soon he was as busy as they. He dug holes in the wet bank with a stick and poked the crawfish out. He put them in the cans the Indian children had brought. Harry and Lily grinned, but did not say much. Then Orvie began to throw water up on the clay bank. "Let's slide," he said to Harry.

The boys ran to the top and slid down the slippery clay bank. Lily followed. The Indian children's old ragged clothes and Orvie's overalls were soon colored red from the sticky clay.

"Come on and slide!" Lily called the other girls. "It's fun."

"We gotta go home," replied Edna Belle Murray.

"Before Mama comes after us," added Nellie Jo.

"Fraidy cats!" called Orvie.

"Water bite 'em," chuckled Harry Big Bear.

"Let's put mud on their dresses," said Lily Wild Berry.

Harry and Orvie and Lily splashed water and threw balls of mud. Addie stood in the water and watched.

The Murray girls shrieked and when they saw mud on their dresses and aprons, began to cry. They stumbled off through the thicket of brush and briars.

"They'll tell their Mama on you, Orvie," said Addie.

"Don't care if they do," said Orvie. "They're such fraidy cats, I always like to scare 'em and make 'em run."

"Me too," chuckled Harry Big Bear.

"Pretty dresses dirty now," said Lily, smiling with satisfaction.

"Let's go home, Orvie," said Addie, picking up her shoes and stockings.

The Indian children took their cans and went off to their home in the Reservation. Orvie and Addie left the shade of the trees and came out on the prairie.

"Let's take a short-cut," said Orvie. They climbed a fence.

"There's Grandpa!" cried Addie happily.

They hurried to catch up with him.

"Well, well, where you kids been?" Grandpa Robinson's brown, weathered face crinkled with a warm smile. His lean figure was dressed in his worn everyday overalls. He carried a rifle in one hand, and held a couple of jackrabbits in the other.

"Where'd you shoot 'em, Grandpa?" demanded Orvie.

"Ain't you a sight, Grandpa!" cried Addie. "Mama'll sure

scold you for shootin' jackrabbits on Sunday."

"Your Mama'll be glad to get the makin's of a good rabbit stew," laughed Grandpa.

"Maybe Aunt Lottie and Uncle Mart will be gone by the time we get home," said Orvie. "Mama always scolds worse when they're at our house."

"They like to get all the good meals they can," said Grandpa. "They won't leave before supper, mark my words."

"You haven't told us where you been, Grandpa," said Orvie.

"Over to that wildcat oil well," replied the old man. "I tried to bring you a dog, Orvie, but he got away. He was wild as a wolf and half-starved. I found a piece of rope and tried to drag him home, but he broke loose and I couldn't catch him. A wild dog like that—I could train him to chase jackrabbits."

"Wish you'da caught him, Grandpa," said Orvie.

They crossed the pasture and entered the barn lot from the rear. Grandpa hung the jackrabbits up on a limb of the cotton-wood tree and put his rifle in his house. Suddenly a dog with shaggy hair appeared beside the barn.

"There he is now," said Grandpa. "Here Shep, here Shep!" But the dog would not come near.

"Is his name Shep?" asked Addie.

"Yes," said Grandpa. "He belonged to those oil drillers before they abandoned that dry hole. He was just a stray puppy, but they took to feedin' him and he stayed around the well. Since they went off, he's got skinny and half-starved, with nobody to feed him."

"I'll get him something to eat," said Orvie. He ran in the back kitchen door and came out with a pan of milk, and some bones.

[8]

"The folks are still there," he said, "all sittin' on the front porch visitin'. Aunt Lottie's still talkin'." He set the food down on the ground.

"We'd better leave him alone for a few days," said Grandpa, "till he gets used to us."

They went inside Grandpa's house. He had a bed, a bureau, a table and a chair. All three sat down on the bed. The dog drank the milk and chewed the bones between growls. Then he slunk away. Grandpa came out and began to clean the jackrabbits.

"Ding, dong! Ding, dong!" rang the farm bell.

"There's Della on the back porch, ringing the bell for supper," said Addie. She poured water from Grandpa's pitcher, and they all washed in his bowl.

They went in to supper, and there was Bert, fifteen, Della, seventeen, Papa and Mama, Aunt Lottie and Uncle Mart. They folded their hands while Papa said grace. Sunday night supper was always good, because it was everything left over from Sunday dinner—chicken and mashed potatoes and coleslaw and a big dish of gravy, pie and cakes, preserves, pickles and jelly.

At first nobody said much because they were so busy passing the food around and helping themselves. Then their mouths were so full they could not talk. The way Aunt Lottie and Mama kept looking at Grandpa's overalls and saying nothing made Orvie uncomfortable. Grandpa's daughters-in-law had a hard time making him behave. No wonder he had bought a brooder house and moved his bedroom furniture in, so he could live by himself and be his own boss. Orvie decided he would do the same when he grew up. He wouldn't have a bunch of women telling him what to do.

[9]

"I sure do miss them oil drillers," began Grandpa. When he was full of good food, Grandpa loved to talk.

Mama looked at Aunt Lottie as if to say, "So that's where he's been, and on Sunday too."

"It was company to set up there nights and listen to that radio that Slim rigged up," Grandpa went on. "That young feller was smart. First he made a contraption he called a 'crystal set,' but them ear phones hurt my ears. He kept tinkerin' at it, but couldn't get it to work very well. Then he got an Atwater Kent with a loud speaker . . ."

"Yes," said Mama. "Ear-splittin' thing—we could hear it a mile away. You and Old Pickering and those other men set up there from six in the evenin' till one-two in the mornin'—listenin' and gassin'. I was awful glad when those drillers moved off."

"An old man needs to get his proper sleep," put in Aunt Lottie bitingly, "and at night-time too, not all day long."

"Oh, I can sleep any old time," laughed Grandpa.

"Guess they've given up the idea of striking oil," said Uncle Mart, trying to be agreeable. He had a round genial face and was short and comfortably stout. "They got tired of payin' a yearly rental on that lease."

"The lease ran out," said Grandpa. "They'll come along some day and renew it."

"Somebody's always getting a notion there's a sea of oil under the state of Oklahoma," said Papa. "I'm tired of waiting for 'em to find it."

"When they do, can I get a piano and take music lessons?" asked Della.

Everybody laughed. "Don't count your chickens before they are hatched, Della," said Uncle Mart.

Grandpa pushed back his chair, wiped his mouth and thrust a toothpick in. "I'm confident we'll get oil right here one day

before I die," he said. "The good Lord revealed it to me thirty years ago."

The two women raised their eyebrows. "There he goes again!" whispered Lottie to Jennie.

"I been predictin' it for thirty years, ever since I took my claim," Grandpa went on.

"What makes you think so?" asked Uncle Mart.

"The lay of the land looks like oil lays under it, to my notion," said Grandpa.

Everybody laughed, even Bert and Della.

"Oh Pa, stop your foolish talk," said Mama.

"That driller—Slim Rogers his name was—give me his confidence," Grandpa went on. "He asked me to store his tools, when they abandoned that well for a dry hole. In the two years they was drillin', they went down two thousand feet. Some day they'll go deeper'n that. He told me confidentially never to sell this farm, because there's oil under it."

"You shoulda sold it long ago and bought a better farm where we could at least make a livin'," began Mama bitterly.

"No ma'm!" Grandpa sat up with a jerk. "I made the Run in '93 and I picked out this quarter-section and I've hung onto it for thirty years and I won't never give it up. Even if it's not so good for farmin', we might strike oil . . ."

"And get rich, Grandpa?" Orvie burst in.

"Sure, boy, sure!" Grandpa beamed.

"*I* believe you, Grandpa, even if nobody else does," said the boy.

"So do I, Grandpa," said Addie.

"If you expect to keep the farm, why did you give Old Pickering that mortgage?" demanded Aunt Lottie.

"Well, I thought I'd invest in oil stock in Texas and get enough to pay him back again and have plenty left over," said Grandpa in a feeble voice.

"Instead of which you lost every cent," said Aunt Lottie accusingly. "Now instead of your son inheriting the farm, Old Pickering'll foreclose and get it."

"No, he won't!" answered Grandpa sharply. "So far Al and me has met all the payments. Before he forecloses, we'll strike oil . . . ."

"*When* he forecloses, where's Al and Jennie and their four children gonna live?" asked Aunt Lottie. "They can't come and sponge on us, nor you neither."

Aunt Lottie was a little woman with a thin, sharp face and a high-pitched voice. Mama looked like her, except that she was plumper and kinder. And Mama's voice was softer, even when she was cross.

"What's done's done and can't be undone," said Mama. Even she and Papa got tired of Aunt Lottie's carping.

"That drouth in the spring ruined last year's wheat crop," said Papa. "Just dried it up to thin straw that wasn't worth cuttin'."

"Those three cows struck by lightning last month didn't help us much," said Mama. "I'll never forget how I found 'em when I went out to the pasture, struck down on their knees right where they were standing. They had to be hauled off and buried. We coulda had a lot of good eating from three cows."

"Three cows less to milk," said Orvie with a grin. "What do we keep so many cows and horses for? I'm sick to death of pumping water for 'em when the wind don't blow."

Bert had been sitting silently, stuffing cake into his mouth. He turned and said crossly: "How can you farm without cows and horses?"

"Get a tractor!" shouted Orvie. "You don't have to feed and water a tractor."

"Tractors don't give milk," said Bert angrily.

"Tractors cost money," said Papa.

They all got up from the supper table. Aunt Lottie and Uncle Mart went into the bedroom to get their hats to go.

"We'll get money yet," said Grandpa, rubbing his hands together. "We'll get it the easy way—oil, oil, oil!"

CHAPTER II

No. 1 Murray

"Orvie! Orvie!"

Orvie turned over in bed sleepily. But the voice kept on calling. He raised up, took one look at Bert still asleep beside him, then slid out of bed.

"Orvie! Orvie!" called Papa's voice again.

"I'm comin'." Pulling his clothes on hastily, the boy ran down the stairs and out into the yard.

It was early morning and the sun was rising. He hurried to the barn and jumped on the pony, whose name was Star. He rode off over the prairie to round up the work horses that had been grazing all night in the wheat field.

It was February, still winter, and the air was cold. The darkness of night was breaking away, giving place to the pink glow of dawn. The sky looked so big and vast and open, it gave Orvie a wonderful sense of freedom. The family were still asleep. Even Papa was taking a last-minute doze.

A boy alone on a pony, alone on the big wide prairie—it was worth being roused out of sound sleep; it was the grandest time in the whole day. It was wonderful just to be alive. Orvie lay down on Star's back and let her go where she wanted to go. Then he sat up suddenly.

He imagined he was Buffalo Bill. He saw a movement in the bushes and was certain it was a buffalo. No—it was only a coyote. He wished he had brought Grandpa's rifle. There weren't any more buffalo—he knew that. He thought of the great herds that used to graze on the Oklahoma prairies, and of the herds of cattle that used to be driven by cowboys on trails from Texas to Kansas City. He was born too late—he had missed all the fun.

He saw something on the ground, pulled the pony up and slid off. It was a buffalo skull, bleached white, with jet black horns —mute evidence of a vanished herd. If he scraped the horns and polished them, he wondered if Mama would let him hang it up in the house for a hat rack. He mounted Star, holding the skull in front of him.

He saw a movement in the bushes again. Now there were two coyotes—they had been out prowling for chickens. He rode fast to race them to their hole. Then he saw a third animal racing with them. It was Shep, who had grown tame and plump after living with the Robinson family all winter. *"Shep, Shep! Come here, Shep!"* he called. But the dog did not come. Grandpa was right—he was wild as a wolf. Dog and coyotes disappeared in a thicket of blackjack oaks.

[16]

The horses were in the farthest corner of the field as always. Orvie drove them in, put the buffalo skull in the barn and forgot about it. He had seen something else—a strange man in the field not far from the side road. The man had parked his car and climbed over the barbed wire fence. He was walking about in a strange manner.

Orvie hurried through breakfast and told Grandpa. "There was a man out in the wheat field," he said. "I couldn't figure out what he was doin'."

"We'll go investigate," said Grandpa.

The man was back of the barn now. He was dressed in city clothes and he acted excited. He introduced himself.

"My name's Witherspoon, Harvey E.," he said briskly. "See what I got?" He dangled a string with a bulging leather sack on the end. "Some folks make fun of me and call this a 'doodle-bug!' When I hold it just the right way and make certain movements, the sack will go round and round. Others use witch sticks, the same as for water, but my method is my own invention and if there's oil . . ."

"OIL!" gasped Grandpa. "Are you locatin' OIL?"

"Sure as shootin', mister!" The man's eyes gleamed fiercely.

"Golly!" exclaimed Orvie. "What you got in that sack?"

The man glared at Orvie and said, "I can't tell you."

Grandpa cleared his throat. Then he spoke softly: "Do you think there's oil on this place?"

"Just wait a minute. Be very still now," said Harvey E. Witherspoon. He stopped suddenly by a puddle near the pigpen. He stood still, held his sack up by the string and waited, his bright eyes fixed on the sack. He seemed to be saying words to himself. Orvie and Grandpa watched, all eyes fixed on the sack.

Then it happened. The string began to vibrate and the sack turned round and round. No one said a word until Witherspoon moved.

"There's oil right *here*!" He pointed to the puddle. "Tell them to drill on this exact spot. Get a stake, boy, and pound it in. Does this farm belong to you, mister?"

"Yes," said Grandpa solemnly. "My name's Robinson, Orville J. Sr." He reached in his pocket and gave all the money he had to the stranger. "When we strike oil, you come back and I'll give you some more."

"Thanks," said Witherspoon, flushing.

Although they did not know it, the doodlebugger was the first of many strange visitors to the Robinson farm. As Grandpa and Orvie walked back to the house, Grandpa was visibly trembling. "At last, at last," he kept saying. They stopped at the edge of the yard.

"Better not say a word to anybody about the doodlebugger, Orvie," warned Grandpa. "They might not understand."

"I wasn't going to," said Orvie. "I got sense enough for that."

[18]

The next day after school Mama sent Orvie to the country store at Cloverleaf Corners, a mile and a quarter from the Robinson farmhouse. Mama was out of coffee and sugar and wanted them quickly. Orvie walked fast and it did not take him long to get there.

The store was the only building at the four corners. It had a board sidewalk and a high false front. A narrow door opened between two wide show windows. Inside, a number of people were lounging about, talking. Orvie saw Harry Big Bear. "Hi!" he called.

Harry was sitting on a small barrel, hunched over, staring at the floor. His grandfather, White Cloud, was talking to the proprietor. Orvie glanced up at the sign on the wall and read it over:

"Peg-Leg Moore Runs This Store
Don't Spit on the Floor—Open the Door."

Peg-Leg's real name was Henry, but nobody used it. Ever since he had been in a railroad wreck and lost his leg, he had been nicknamed Peg-Leg. He had made his wooden leg himself because it was cheaper than a factory one. Peg-Leg was bald and wore glasses. His wooden leg made a brisk tapping on the floor as he pattered about. Now he stood behind the counter, looking at White Cloud over his glasses. "What's that you say?"

"Just ten dollars . . . to bury my baby . . ." said White Cloud in a mournful voice. The Indian wore overalls, his big black felt hat had a small feather on one side, and braids of black hair hung down at each side of his dark brown face.

"Not today," laughed Peg-Leg. "You Otoe Indians will soon

[19]

be gettin' rich like the Osages from selling oil leases. Then you can bury all your dead babies and lend *us* money."

The Indian's expression did not change. "My poor baby . . ."

"Your Grandpa got oil?" Orvie hurried over to ask Harry. "You gonna get rich?"

But Harry Big Bear did not answer as he followed White Cloud out of the store.

The people in the store were all talking. Orvie heard the word "oil" on every tongue.

"The Indians may get the money," laughed Jess Woods, a farmer, "but the white men won't let them keep it long."

"Money ain't everything, but it helps!" said Hank Newton.

A cluster of women had gathered in a corner. "She'll soon be sittin' pretty," said one. "She'll soon be buyin' new furniture." "She's awful close—good at pinchin' pennies," said another. "Do you think they'll move to town?" inquired the third.

"Who were they talking about?" Orvie asked Peg-Leg, when he began to make his purchases. "Somebody come into money?"

"Gosh, boy, where you been? Haven't you heard the news?" replied the storekeeper. "The whole countryside's talkin' about it. There's a rumor they've got a showing of oil on the Murray place. That's right up there by you folks—next quarter-section, ain't it?"

"Golly, yes!" gasped Orvie. "The Murrays are our nearest neighbors on the west, only half a mile away."

"You didn't know?" asked Peg-Leg.

"We knew they started drilling before Christmas and the drillers nearly froze to death, but everybody said it would be a dry hole like that wildcat well by the creek. Are the Murrays gonna be rich?"

"It looks that way," said Peg-Leg. "Of course they've only had a showing of oil. They're drilling through one sand till they come to the next. Meanwhile, leases and royalties are being bought up in all directions. It looks like good times are coming all right."

Orvie could hardly wait till he got home to tell the news. "They said at the store the Murrays are gonna get oil!" he announced.

"The Murrays!" exclaimed Mama. "I can't believe it."

"I'm glad if they do," said Papa. "They've worked hard, they deserve it."

"I wonder if Lena Murray will get her improvements," said Mama, "running water, a bathroom and electric lights. She sure needs them."

On his way home from school the next day, Orvie stopped at

the Murray farm to see their oil well. Edna Belle and Nellie Jo came out and watched for a while, but their mother soon called them back in. There was no one else around but the workmen.

The wooden derrick had a long covered passageway at one side, which sheltered the steam engine. The machinery was pumping away and the men did not seem to be very busy. One of them came up and answered Orvie's questions. He took him in the "doghouse"—a shelter for the men—and let him watch from there. He explained that the steam engine turned the band wheel, which in turn operated the walking beam. The walking beam, a huge arm on top of the sturdy Sampson post, raised and lowered the long cable tools in the well, with the drill bit on the end. Each stroke meant that the well was getting deeper. The derrick or rig was built to support the drilling machinery, and also the long joints of casing pipe with which the well hole must be lined.

Orvie hadn't been there long before Grandpa arrived with Shep. "Thought I'd better keep track of what's going on over here," said Grandpa.

A car drove up and a young man jumped out. Grandpa hurried to meet him with outstretched hand. "Well, if it ain't my old friend, Slim Rogers."

"Gosh almighty!" cried Slim. "If it ain't Grandpap Robinson and my old dog Shep." He bent over the dog, who began to bark and wag his tail. "Been feedin' him, have you?"

"Orvie has," said Grandpa. "This is my grandson, Orville, Jr."

"Pleased to meet you." Slim smiled down at the boy.

"You workin' here with this outfit?" asked Grandpa.

"No, I'm tyin' up with the Sooner Oil Company, I think."

"I thought you'd gone off to Texas or Louisiana or some other oil field," said Grandpa. "It does a feller's eyes good to see you again. Come over to the house and have supper with us some day."

"Sure will," said Slim. "How's that pretty granddaughter of yours?"

"Prettier'n a rose in summertime," laughed Grandpa. "Della says when oil strikes, she'll get a piano and take music lessons. But her folks are bound and determined there'll never be no oil on that farm of mine."

Slim lowered his voice. "Remember what I told you before I left here? You'll get oil sure enough. You sold your lease to . . ."

Grandpa nodded. "Sure! Months ago. I'm all fixed."

Slim smiled.

"Are they gettin' oil for the Murrays?" asked Grandpa.

"They'll know for sure in a day or two," said Slim.

After that, things began to happen fast.

There was the day when the "rock hounds" wandered over Grandpa's farm. They stopped at the house and said they were geologists, sent by the oil company to locate oil. They called their instrument a seismograph or earthquake instrument, and explained that they had to bury dynamite to make an underground explosion. By listening to these earthquake waves, they hoped to locate soft rocks which might hold oil.

"Jerusalem!" exclaimed Grandpa. "Sounds like a lot of trouble. Now Harvey E. Witherspoon had a doodlebug, and another fellow had a witch stick and they both insist that there is oil right under my barn lot."

But the geologists did not listen to the doodlebuggers or to

Grandpa. They wandered over the fields and roads, tied mysterious red and white rags to wire fences, and talked very little.

One day they came near the barn lot and set off an explosion which broke all the eggs in the henhouse and two of the kitchen windows. Papa ran to chase the men off. They tried to explain that they might find oil for him.

"Get out!" shouted Papa. "I'm tired of this oil talk—nothing comes of it."

Then the "royalty peddlers" began to pester Grandpa, and he had to go to Slim again for advice. The whole family soon learned that the company that buys the lease is entitled to seven-eighths of the royalty that the sale of the oil brings, while the land owner keeps one-eighth of it. Of this one-eighth royalty, the owner can decide to sell as many acres as he chooses.

The previous fall, Grandpa Robinson had sold the lease on his farm to the Sooner Oil Company for two thousand dollars cash, which was more money than he had seen in his entire life. He had hitched the team of horses to the wagon and driven to Tonkawa, seven miles north, where he had deposited the check in the bank. But he had told no one.

The Sunday after they heard the rumor about the Murray well, Aunt Lottie and Uncle Mart came to spend the day. Even Orvie and little Addie noticed the change in Aunt Lottie. She didn't scold Grandpa once. She went out to his little house, swept it clean and made up his bed with fresh sheets. She brought his kerosene lamp into the kitchen, filled it and shined the chimney.

"I think it's a shame, Jennie," she said, "the way you treat your father-in-law—chasing him outside and making him live in a hen-house."

"It was his idea, not mine," answered Mama. "I told him the neighbors would talk, and he said he wanted to give them something extry good to talk about. You know how stubborn he is—he won't listen to anybody."

"We'll have to make him move back in," said Aunt Lottie. "How will it look if he comes into a lot of oil money—him living out there as if he'd quarreled with his son and daughter-in-law?"

That day, at Sunday dinner and supper, all the talk was of leases and royalties. Bert got tired of it and left the table before the meal was half through. Aunt Lottie and Uncle Mart hinted and hinted, but Grandpa was silent all through the meal. He kept his eyes glued on his plate, ate fast, and when he had finished, pushed a toothpick in his mouth and stalked out of the room.

"He don't need to tell us," snorted Lottie. "We know already."

"He got two thousand for that lease," said Uncle Mart. "The man at the bank told me."

"Two thousand!" gasped Mama. "Do you think he's been selling royalties too?"

They did not know, but, acting on Slim's advice, Grandpa had been speculating carefully. The first twenty acres of royalty he had sold in the early spring at five dollars per acre, and had made up his mind to hold all the rest. Later, he had decided that in the event there might be no oil on his place after all, he wanted to be better fixed than he was. So he sold twenty more acres for fifty dollars each. All this money he had deposited in the Tonkawa bank. Lottie and Mart went home that Sunday without finding out this information.

On Wednesday of the week following, Grandpa asked Slim to come down to the house for dinner. Della heaped Slim's plate high, and passed the biscuits frequently. After dinner Grandpa and Slim had a talk. That afternoon, Grandpa sold another twenty acres royalty for two hundred dollars an acre, but he told no one.

The very next day the Murray well struck oil.

The Robinsons were at the supper table when the well blew in. When they heard the explosion, they jumped from their chairs and ran to the back kitchen door.

Across the prairie, green with wheat, they could see the Murray farm buildings silhouetted against the sky. Behind the barn stood the oil derrick, clothed now in a white cloud of gas fumes. As they looked, the gas faded away and oil, like a fountain of muddy water, shot up into the sky. The fountain kept on playing into the night.

The Robinsons looked at each other and they looked at Grandpa, wondering what it meant. They had no idea then how it would change their lives. Only Bert was unconcerned. He had gone out to milk the cows.

"Is that oil?" cried Orvie. "I never knew it would shoot up like that." Not till he saw Grandpa streaking off across the wheat field, heading for the Discovery well, did the boy realize what was happening.

"Golly, OIL!" he exclaimed.

He ran after Grandpa as fast as he could go.

CHAPTER III

No. 1 Pickering

"WHERE'S that dog of yours, Orvie?" called Mama. It was early morning and she was out in the chicken yard, feeding the chickens.

"I haven't seen him, Mama," said Orvie. *"Shep! Shep!"*

"Just look here," said Mama. "Ten chickens gone, maybe more judgin' from the feathers. The coyotes came in the night and grabbed the hens right under Shep's nose and he never barked once."

"I heard a pack of 'em yappin' and yellin'," said Grandpa.

"Where's that dog?" asked Mama. "You go bring him here, Orvie, and give him a good thrashing. He's got to be trained some time."

"Aw, Mama . . . I don't want to," said Orvie.

"Do as I tell you," ordered Mama.

"*Shep! Here Shep!*" called Orvie. "*Shep, Shep, come Shep!* He don't come when I call him, Mama. *Shep, here Shep.*"

"He's run off to the woods with the coyotes," said Grandpa.

Shep had escaped a thrashing this time, and Orvie was glad. He looked and saw a wagon stop in front of the house. "There's Old Pickering, Grandpa."

"Bring your gun, Robinson," shouted Pickering. "I seen a coyote go under the culvert. Let's go shoot 'em out." He drove on.

"We'll get rid of 'em for you," said Grandpa to Mama.

Grandpa got his rifle and walked beside Orvie on the red clay road. The sun was warm and the blue sky was dotted with fleecy clouds. Spring came early in Oklahoma. The pastures would soon be covered with fresh, tender green, and sprinkled with wild flowers.

"Maybe we can take the little ones home and tame 'em," said Orvie.

"Better ketch 'em first," said Grandpa.

"Pickering won't want 'em, will he?"

"He'll sure want the old coyote for the hide," said Grandpa. "Anything with money tied to it, he can smell a mile off."

Old Man Pickering was at the crossroads waiting. He took the gun from Grandpa's hands without delay. He got down in the ditch, took aim and fired under the culvert. Smoke came puffing out as the shot echoed over the prairie.

"I got her," he said. "Crawl in there and pull her out, bub."

Orvie crawled into the round drainage tile and dragged the dead mother coyote out by the legs. His pants became soaked with water and mud but he did not notice.

"There's a whole slew of young ones!" he exclaimed.

"Bring 'em out," said Grandpa.

"Sure, bring 'em out," said Pickering, lifting the dead animal into his wagon.

Orvie brought the young ones out two at a time. They were little and helpless and cute. There were seven in all.

"Can I have . . ." he began.

Old Pickering placed two young coyotes in his wagon. "They're not good for nothing, except to eat chickens. You don't want 'em," he replied.

"Hold on there, Walt," snapped Grandpa. "Who do these critters belong to, anyhow?"

"I located 'em and told you they was here," said Pickering angrily.

"It was my rifle killed the old one," said Grandpa.

"If you was a real neighbor, you'd be willing to lend a gun," said Pickering, "specially when you know mine's broke."

"Yes, I lend my gun, and you take the hide and get the bounty for it," said Grandpa. "Now you're tryin' to take the whole kit'n'boodle of young ones. You always was the grabbin' kind, Walt Pickering, ever since I first seen you. You was a Sooner in '93 and squatted on the land I had picked out for my claim. I took second choice to keep from fightin' you, and you been tryin' to get my farm away from me ever since. You lent me money and I couldn't pay it back, so you took my south eighty. You lent me money on my other eighty, and now you're fixin' to foreclose the mortgage and get it all for your own."

Grandpa lowered his voice so Orvie could not hear. "But I got a surprise for you. Will you meet me at the Tonkawa bank tomorrow morning at ten o'clock?"

Pickering looked startled for a minute, then answered, "Sure." He had placed four of the baby coyotes in his wagon. He reached down and picked up two more.

"Give them two to Orvie," said Grandpa in a sharp voice.

"I was just a-goin' to," said Pickering sheepishly. "I was fixin' to give him all three." He reached for the last one and put the three animals in Orvie's hands. Then he climbed in his wagon and drove down the road without looking back. Orvie put two of the coyotes into his coat pockets and carried the third in his hands. When he got home, he put them in a box.

The next afternoon, he made a wire pen for the coyotes. As he put them in it, he happened to look up at the sky. The next minute he went tearing into the house.

"Mama, there's a big black cloud comin' up in the west," he shouted. "The wind's blowin' like all get out."

Mama put her iron back on the stove to heat and hung Della's freshly-ironed dress on the clothes rack. The wood stove had the words "Solid Comfort" on the oven door, but the kitchen was much too hot for comfort. It felt like a bake oven.

Mama glanced outdoors. "Maybe a rain will clear the air a little."

A sharp gust of wind swept through the kitchen. It rattled windows and banged doors all over the house.

"Della, shut the windows," Mama called. "It's going to rain hard. Orvie, call the men in from the barn. No—you'd better help me get the baby chicks in first. I'll ring the dinner bell. They'll hear it and come in."

Mama went out and pulled the rope. The sharp clangs of the farm bell rang out over the blustering wind.

"My white kitty, it'll get drownded," wailed Addie.

"You stay in the house, Addie," said Mama, "or the wind will blow you away. Here, Orvie, help me." They lifted the pens of baby chicks and carried them into the kitchen. "Orvie, the brake on the windmill. It'll get blown to pieces . . ."

"Bert'll do that, Mama," said Orvie. "I'll just get my coyotes." He rushed out the door.

The sky was getting darker and it began to pour rain.

"My kitty, my kitty . . ." screamed Addie.

"Hush up your bawlin'," said Mama. "Della! *Del*-la! Come quick! We better go in the cave. Looks like a bad storm—no tellin' what this wind might do . . ."

The sky was now dark and threatening. The black cloud was moving fast. A sharp streak of lightning cut across the sky. It was followed by a clap of thunder and loud roaring of the wind.

"Where's Bert and Papa?" cried Della. "And Orvie?"

"Where's Grandpa?" cried Addie.

Mama stooped to pick the white kitten up from its box under the porch and gave it to Addie. She took Della by one hand and Addie by the other. Bending against the wind, they made a dash for the storm cellar, a heap of masonry covered with a mound of dirt, ten feet away from the back porch. But even in that ten feet, they were drenched to the skin, for the rain was now coming down in torrents. Fortunately the sloping door of the cave was open. The three stumbled down the steps.

"Orvie! Orvie! why don't Orvie come?" wailed Addie. "And Grandpa? Where's Grandpa?"

The storm cellar has not been used for a long time except for storage. They stepped over empty fruit jars and earthen crocks. They splashed into the water that covered the dirt floor.

"Oh, there's snakes down here!" cried Della in alarm. "There's frogs and snakes. They'll get on us."

"You hush! You hush up, a big girl like you," scolded Mama.

The next minute Orvie was there, his arms full of coyotes, and Shep following after him.

"Don't you bring them wild critters near me," cried Della. "They'll bite."

"You found that good-for-nothing Shep, I see," said Mama. "Go up and shut the cellar door, Orvie."

"Here, you hold 'em." The boy dumped the animals into Mama's apron.

When the heavy door clanged down it was pitch dark in the cave. The little group could not see the masonry walls nor the arched masonry ceiling. They stood ankle deep in the muddy

water and waited in darkness.

"Wish I'da brung the lantern," said Orvie.

"Old Pickering borrowed it," said Mama, "and forgot to bring it back. Here, take these critters. I don't want to be bit to pieces."

But before Orvie could get hold of them, the three coyotes had slipped out of Mama's apron and had fallen in the water.

"Gosh! They'll get drownded," said Orvie.

"They'll bite my feet," screamed Addie.

Suddenly a crash was heard, muffled yet plain. Mama and the children forgot snakes and coyotes, wondering what it was.

"It's dark down here," wailed Addie. "I'm scared, Mama."

Mama put her arms around the little girl. "We'll go up in a minute."

Then Papa opened the door, looked down and smiled. "Any family of mine down here? Where you folks been hiding?"

It was all over when they came up. The ground was white with hailstones and the air was cold. Shep barked and pranced, Addie's kitten was put safely back in its box, but the three baby coyotes were dead. The house was there—it had not been blown away. The barn and farm buildings were still standing too.

"Bet we lost our wheat again," said Papa. "You watch your wheat grow all winter, then a hailstorm can take it in a single day."

"It don't seem to be hurt none," said Bert coming in from the field. "Good thing the wheat wasn't any higher."

"Guess we're lucky this time, Al," said Mama. "Wonder what that crash was we heard."

They went to look at the house. The hail had made holes in window and door screens, and the paint on the back of the house

[34]

had been taken off in a million spots, where the hail had peppered it. All the window panes on the west side were broken. The floors inside were covered with broken glass and water. The back kitchen door had been left open and the fire in the stove was out.

Orvie forgot about the dead coyotes as he and Addie ran around the yard gathering up hailstones.

"Just see what a mess we got to clean up," grumbled Della, "and all of us soaked to the skin."

"There's always something . . ." began Papa.

"Where's Grandpa?" Addie suddenly asked. *"Grandpa! Grandpa!"*

"He wasn't in the barn with us," said Papa.

The door of the hen-coop under the cottonwood tree opened and Grandpa stepped out. "Did somebody call me? Is it supper time?" He noticed the cool air and saw the hailstones on the ground. "What's happened?"

"Didn't you know we had a bad hailstorm?" asked Orvie, holding up hailstones for him to see. "And we all went down in the cave?"

"Gosh, no," said Grandpa. "I musta dozed off for a little nap. I was tired out from my trip to Tonkawa this morning."

"Always sleepin' in the daytime," said Mama. "You'd sleep through an earthquake. Just see all the damage . . ."

She stopped abruptly, for there on the back porch stood Mrs. Pickering. They had all been too busy thinking of their own troubles to give thought to anybody else. There was Liza Pickering, shawl over her head, crying. Grandpa went back into his hen-coop and shut the door.

[35]

"What's the matter, Liza?" Mama ran to her at once. "Can I help you?"

Liza Pickering was the wife of Walt Pickering, who held Grandpa's mortgage. She was much older than Mama, but they were good friends in spite of the men's differences.

"Come in the kitchen and have a chair," said Mama. "I'll find some dry wood and build up the fire. It's turned cold—fire'll feel good."

"Did the hailstorm hurt you folks?" asked Papa.

Liza sat down and sniffled a bit. "It blew our roof full of holes," she said. "Walt coulda reroofed it long ago, but he wouldn't. He's gonna sell the place, he says, soon as the oil boom starts. He's got a buyer all set to buy it. It's been my home since we first built our sod-house there in '93 and I don't want to leave . . ."

"But the hailstorm, Liza," inquired Mama. "Is that all it did—blew holes in your roof?"

"The oil derrick blew over . . ." began Liza.

"That must have been the crash we heard," said Papa.

"It fell on my chicken coop and smashed it flat and killed all my chickens and Walt had left our Ford out and it fell smack on it and mashed it flat too." Liza began crying again.

"What do you care about that old Ford, Liza?" said Mama. "You got all that lease money to buy you a new one. And when you strike oil, you can buy all the cars you want. You'll be sittin' pretty!"

The No. 1 Pickering well had been started by a second oil company a short time after the No. 1 Murray had begun drilling. But it had had many setbacks, and this was one more.

Liza kept on crying.

"They'll set the rig right up again," Papa encouraged her. "They'll be drilling again in no time."

"I know they will," said Liza between sobs. "That's what gets me. They'll set it up and they'll strike oil and Walt'll get an awful lot of money, and you know what he's gonna do with it?"

"No, what?" asked Mama.

"He's gonna sell our house to a roadhouse man for a dance hall!" said Liza. "You folks won't like that, but I thought I better tell you."

"Oh no—surely he wouldn't do that!" gasped Mama and Papa together.

"And instead of buyin' me a fine house to live in, in town, he's going to start a filling station down by Cloverleaf Corners, and we have to live upstairs."

"Well, of all things!" exclaimed Mama.

Mrs. Pickering left, and Mama watched her bent figure go trudging down the road.

"Nobody was glad when Old Pickering got three thousand for his lease," said Papa. "He's been such an old money-grabber all along."

"You never could tell they had all that money to look at them," said Mama. "Walt hasn't had a new suit or Liza a new dress for ten years—they're that tight."

"The more Pickering gets, the more he wants," said Papa. "He'll take Pa's farm right out from under us and then what'll we do?"

"I hate him," said Orvie. "Never has a pleasant word for nobody. After what he done to Grandpa, gettin' Grandpa's south eighty, and tryin' to get the whole farm . . ."

"Your Grandpa wasn't obliged to borrow money off him, son," said Papa.

"Oh, your Pa and his fool schemes," mourned Mama. "Always figurin' on gettin' rich buyin' oil stock . . ." Mama lowered her voice. "Has he told you, Al, what he got for our lease? Mart says two thousand. Why don't he pay Old Pickering off, and keep our home for us? If he was like other men, he'd give his son half the royalty right now, so you wouldn't have to wait till he dies . . ."

In walked Grandpa. Mama's voice faded and she set to work energetically sweeping out the broken glass and water.

"She gone? The old lady gone?" asked Grandpa.

"Old Pickering's not gonna get our farm, is he, Grandpa?" asked Orvie.

[38]

"Not on your life!" said Grandpa in a loud voice.

Papa and Mama and Della and even little Addie looked up. There was a firm ring in Grandpa's voice that had not been there before.

"I've paid him off in cold cash!" announced Grandpa. "And I've bought back my south eighty. Now I've got my whole quarter-section, my original claim from the Cherokee Strip."

"Golly, Grandpa!" cried Orvie. "I knew you would!"

"Grandpa! Why, Grandpa!" exclaimed the family.

"I been intendin' to tell you," said Grandpa. "I've leased the mineral rights on my farm to the Sooner Oil Company, and I've sold a few royalties here and there. I gave a hundred dollars to the Prairie View Church for a thank-offering. Then I made up my mind the next thing I'd do with my oil money was to pay out my home, so it'll come to you and Al clear and free."

"My land, Pa. This sure is a surprise!" said Mama.

Grandpa leaned over and gave his daughter-in-law a hearty kiss. Then Papa told about the Pickerings' dance hall and filling station.

Grandpa spat out the back door to express his disgust. "Don't surprise me none," he said. "Just like the old weasel."

They talked it all over happily. A great burden had been lifted for everybody. It was wonderful not to be under Pickering's thumb any longer. Grandpa basked in a new kind of glory—everybody respected him now that he had money. That night at supper he sat at the head of the table.

"We'll have to have new window lights and screens, and paint for the house," began Mama.

"I need summer dresses and a new straw hat," said Della.

"The corn crib blew over and the old wagon's broke down," said Papa.

"Windmill's smashed," said Bert. "I tried to anchor it before the storm hit, but the wind was too strong."

Grandpa waved his hand. "Order what you need right away and I'll pay for it."

Orvie brought the mail-order catalogue and leaned against Grandpa's knee. Addie came to look.

"Anything you kids want?" asked Grandpa, smiling.

"A real good bicycle," said Orvie.

"And a pretty doll," said Addie.

Grandpa looked around at the family and grinned. "Too bad Aunt Lottie's not here today!"

"Good thing she's not," said Mama. "She'd make you move back in the house right away."

They all laughed.

CHAPTER IV

Spudding-In

O N THE day when the first oil well was started on Grandpa
Robinson's farm, Orvie was so excited he forgot about
going to school. He followed the men all around. First the location had to be decided.

"My land! Not there!" cried Mama. "Can't you see that's my
rose bed. They'll be a sight next May."

The men with their instruments moved across the lawn to a
spot nearer the fence.

Grandpa hurried out. "Now Harvey E. Witherspoon insisted the exact spot was in the barn lot to the east of the hog
pen . . ."

But the men did not listen. They moved farther down by the
fence.

"Those are my peonies," said Mama firmly.

"Lady, we can't bother about no flower beds," said the man. "We're here to stake a location for this oil well, we've got orders from the company. We got to put it where the geologists tell us we can expect to get oil. You can transplant them flowers, can't you?"

"Peonies won't bloom for two-three years once you move 'em," said Mama tearfully.

"Oh Mama, what do you care about a few old flowers?" said Orvie.

"They're not gonna uproot my peonies," said Mama. "I brought 'em from my mother's garden in Kansas."

"Over the fence then, boys," said the boss.

"In the peach orchard?" cried Mama.

It hardly deserved the name of orchard, for most of the trees had died in the drouth the spring before. But there were three trees left, with a sprinkling of pink blossoms.

"First it's roses you want to keep, then peonies, then peaches!" snorted the man. "Go ahead—lay it off!" he shouted to the men. "Sorry, lady, it can't be helped. Just wait till you see the oil shootin' up, then you'll feel happy again."

Mama covered her face with her apron and cried. Then she went back into the house and watched from a side window. The men hired Papa and other farmers with teams and scrapers to dig the cellar. But first they pulled the peach trees out by the roots.

As the teams dug the hole out, Orvie and Addie ran up and down the slope. Harry Big Bear and Ralph Wilkins, who lived on the next quarter-section north, came to see and join in the excitement.

Grandpa felt better now that he saw the work under way. He sat in a rocking chair on the front porch and watched. Ever since drilling had begun at the No. 1 Pickering well across the road, Grandpa had been fuming about an "offset well" and sputtering about the slowness of the Sooner Oil Company. Sometimes he wondered if he had made a mistake in following Slim Rogers' advice. Maybe some of the other oil companies that had been after him would have acted more quickly. After waiting thirty years for these events to take place, Grandpa was impatient. He wanted the drilling to get under way to compete with No. 1 Pickering.

The cellar was barely dug, and concrete piers set for the derrick, when the material began to roll in.

One day Orvie came home from school by way of Cloverleaf Corners and saw three teams hitched to a single load of oil pipe coming along the road.

The teamster called to him: "Know anybody by the name of Orville J. Robinson Sr. around here? Where does he live?"

"That's my Grandpa," replied Orvie. "My name's Orville J. Robinson Jr., but they call me Orvie."

"My name's Shorty," said the teamster. "Hop up, Orvie, and I'll give you a ride."

The heavy wagon rumbled on, and they were friends at once.

"We're called 'skinners,'—or 'mule skinners' when we drive mules," the man told Orvie.

" 'Skinners?' Why?" asked the boy.

"Now you just watch me," said Shorty. "We gotta whip our horses to make 'em lay down on the pull." He reached for the whip and snapped it viciously over the horses' heads. "When we whip 'em, we take off some hide—we skin 'em, you see. Why, a good skinner can tear a horse to pieces! That's why we're called 'skinners.' "

"Your horses still got plenty of hide on," laughed Orvie. "They ain't been skinned *yet*."

"No, but you just wait . . ."

"Looks to me like you take extry good care of 'em," Orvie went on. "I know enough about horses to tell that. I've lived on a farm all my life, and I don't often see horses so big and strong and sleek-lookin'."

"That so? I can flip a fly from the lead horse's left ear without touchin' the critter," bragged Shorty. "Not one whipcrack in twenty ever touches one of my horses."

"What's that fancy thing around their necks?" asked Orvie.

"That big piece of leather?" asked Shorty. "That's called a 'housing'—it goes over the hames, so rain water won't get under the horses' collars. It protects 'em from heat and cold, too. Us skinners have our names in gold on the housings. Notice that?"

When the teamster stopped in Grandpa's wheat field, Orvie looked. Sure enough, there was the word SCOTT in raised gold letters on the big piece of leather.

"Your name Scott?" asked Orvie.

"Shorty Scott," said the man. "There's five brothers of us, all teamsters. Scott Brothers, you see. We like team work. All the oil companies know us. We haul machinery and casings from Bliss or Tonkawa or Ponca City out to wherever they send us."

Orvie was lost in admiration. He decided it would be wonderful to be a teamster, who was nicknamed a 'skinner,' but who liked his horses too well to ever take the skin off of them.

"Each set of harness on them horses cost me $125," bragged Shorty.

"Whew!" whistled Orvie.

"See all them pretty red and blue celluloid rings for ornament? Each horse has got $40 worth, and each housing cost $22." Shorty pointed out the extra heavy horse shoes, with sharp toes and caulks. "A caulk is a pointed piece on a horseshoe to prevent slipping. They git a new set of shoes once a month."

That evening Shorty let Orvie lead the teams down to the tank at the windmill in the pasture, to water them. Grandpa and Addie went along. The wind was blowing hard from the south and keeping the pump going, so the tank was overflowing. But Orvie was so proud of the handsome horses, he would have pumped a thousand strokes willingly, to water them.

One day, later on, Shorty asked Orvie to ride with him to Bliss to bring the steam boilers. There were four of them and it took ten teams on two wagons to bring them the long distance. Shorty hauled two with five teams.

It began to rain before noon, and the red clay roads soon became wet and muddy. The teams and wagons crawled along, mile after mile, making deeper and deeper ruts in the narrow road. Shorty told Orvie wonderful tales as they rode along, so it did not seem long at all. They were within sight of Moore's Store at Cloverleaf Corners, when the heavy load bogged down in the mud. It was raining hard now and Shorty got out to look.

"That chug hole's deep enough to bury a house in," he said. "You go up to the store and wait, Orvie. You can't help."

Peg-Leg had a fire going in the stove, and there were quite a few people sitting around. Orvie told them all about the latest progress on No. 1 Robinson, and they were all sure that the Sooner Oil Company would strike oil.

Shorty and the other teamster stopped in at the store when they got the wagon out of the hole, and dried their clothes. Soon Orvie was home again, the boilers were unloaded in the wheat field and Shorty's horses were in the corral for the night.

In the days that followed, Orvie could not keep track of all the wagons that came. Heavy loads of pipe, tools and drilling machinery were hauled in and dumped everywhere—over the lawn around the house, in the barn lot, through the peach or-chard and in the adjoining wheat fields. Fences that Papa had put up so carefully were knocked roughly down, as the teams and wagons went where they pleased. Nobody remembered where Mama's rose and peony beds were. They disappeared, trampled under by wheel and hoof.

The steam boilers lay on the ground while the rig was being built, and Orvie and Harry and Ralph had fun crawling through them. Orvie was sorry when the hauling stopped and Shorty Scott and his beautiful teams of horses went away. But he soon forgot them when Gus and the rig-builders came. It was even

[46]

more exciting to see a derrick go up.

"Will you build it as high as the windmill in the pasture?" asked Orvie.

"Ten times higher!" laughed Gus, but Orvie did not believe that.

The pounding and hammering began early each day and Orvie got up early to watch. Mama insisted he must not go on missing so much school, so he had started in again. It was no fun to walk a mile and a half on the back road, where there was no oil excitement at all, and to stay in the lonely school-house with Miss Plumley and a bunch of little children all day long. Orvie told Miss Plumley that he had decided not to be a teamster like Shorty, but a rig-builder like Gus. Miss Plumley didn't even listen. She poked an Arithmetic under the boy's nose, and told him he had to make up all the pages he had missed.

Each night Orvie hurried home to see how high the rig had grown during the day. It seemed to shoot up by leaps and bounds. He felt as if some day it might hit the sky!

The Robinson well was not the only one being started. Others were being located on nearby farms. A lumber company from Tonkawa set up a branch near Cloverleaf Corners. Gus, the rig-builder, told Bert he could get a job at high wages building rigs.

"Would they hire a kid like me?" asked Bert.

"Any man with a weak mind and a strong back can git a job in the oil field," laughed Gus.

Bert decided to try it, but after a week he gave up.

"What's the matter?" asked Mama. "What about all that money you was going to make?"

"I'm too light-headed," Bert said. "I don't like bein' up so

[47]

high in the air."

"You haven't got enough in your head to hold you down," teased Orvie. "Could you see clear over into Kansas and Arkansas?"

"G'wan!" cried Bert impatiently. "I saw one guy fall and that cooked me. I'm going to be a farmer. Don't know why Grandpa had to let that old oil company come in and tear our farm up."

Papa was hired with his team and scraper to scoop out a big slush-pond back of the barn. Then he did other digging for the oil company, to make a little extra money. Bert agreed to take over the milk-route. They could all see that farming was becoming more difficult, but they could still keep on pasturing cows and selling milk. Mama bought more young chickens, so she would have plenty to sell.

The wooden rig rose up only a stone's-throw from the house on the north. The boilers were installed and the drilling machinery set up. The rig-builders went away.

Grandpa had kept his word and ordered a new bicycle for Orvie and a new doll for Addie from the mail-order catalogue. It took them a long time to come and when they did, Orvie and Addie paid little attention to them. For the same day the drillers began the actual drilling.

Orvie and Addie went out with Grandpa to watch. " 'Spudding-in' they call it," Orvie explained.

The steam engine began to thud and the tools were pounding in the black hole in the middle of the derrick floor.

"Addie," shouted Slim above the noise, "we need you up here. Just for luck, won't you wish the well in? If we get oil, you shall have a brand-new silk dress."

[48]

Addie's eyes sparkled. "How do I do it?"

"Lean over the hole and make your wish, but don't tell us what it is." Slim held her as she repeated the old rhyme:

> *"I wish I may, I wish I might*
> *Have the wish I wish tonight."*

Then she closed her eyes and lips and made a solemn wish. Although she did not tell what it was, they all knew that little Addie was wise enough to wish for oil.

"When do I get my silk dress, Slim?" she cried, dancing up and down.

"Not for a while, young lady," laughed Slim.

That first day, the drill hammered its way two hundred feet into the earth. Two hundred feet of twenty-inch pipe was lowered inside the well, to line it.

"My land! Do we have to listen to all that noise?" Mama

complained at dinner time. "Not only the noise but the vibration —it's going to shake the house to pieces. It will break all the windows."

"Now, now Jennie," said Grandpa soothingly. "How can they drill without a little noise and shaking of the machinery? You'll get used to it."

"It's giving me the headache already," said Mama. "Oh, it used to be nice and peaceful around here before all this ruckus started."

"Jennie," said Grandpa sternly. "You been wantin' improvements, haven't you?"

"Yes Pa," said Mama. "Al will never manage to get them. He never has time to fix things around the house. He's always fixin' machinery or mendin' harness."

"This farm has never been worth a row of pins when it comes to crops," Grandpa went on. "Al's Ma and I worked our fingers to the bone and now you and Al are doin' the same thing. But if we can get oil, maybe it will make things easier for us all. But you can't get oil without sufferin' the inconveniences of gettin' it. Understand?"

"Yes, Pa," said Mama meekly.

Della came in. "With all that noise, how's a person to hear herself think?"

"Now you—just like your Mama," said Grandpa. With a twinkle in his eye, he added, "Have you seen that handsome young feller out there at the well?"

"Course not," said Della. "I've got no use for those greasy, grimy fellows. Why any man goes in for oil field work I cannot understand. Gets covered with mud and oil from head to foot.

It's the dirtiest work in the world."

"Here he comes now, Della," said Grandpa. "Better not let him hear what you're sayin'."

The man came up on the back porch following Orvie.

"Here's Slim, Mama, Della! Grandpa, here's Slim!" cried Orvie excitedly.

Della blushed pink when Slim came into the kitchen. Shep dashed up and jumped all over the young man.

"Hey, you old oil field pup!" laughed Slim. "Be a good dog now. Get down, get down."

"He's not much good, Slim," said Orvie. "But we like him anyhow. Are you the driller on our well?"

"No," said Slim. "That big stout fellow—we call him Heavy —he's head driller. I'm his right-hand man, the tool-dresser. But I'll be a driller myself some fine day."

Slim stayed for dinner and told how he had worked in a dozen oil fields all over the United States. He said he liked working for the Sooner Oil Company. He explained all about cable-tool drilling, while Grandpa and Papa and Orvie nodded their heads wisely, but Mama, Della and Bert said they didn't know what he was talking about.

"You'll all learn before you know it," laughed Slim.

That was the beginning of many meals taken in the Robinson home by drillers, tool-dressers and roustabouts. They were good men in spite of their rough ways, eager for friendship and conversation, and they enjoyed Mama's wholesome cooking.

There were two tours (pronounced "towers" in the oil field) or shifts of five men each on the drilling crew. Each tour worked twelve hours a day, seven days a week. The boss of the tour was the driller, who handled the actual operation of the drill. The tool-dresser assisted him in sharpening bits, pulling casing and other jobs. The boilermen operated the boiler, and the roustabouts were laborers for odd chores.

One day when Orvie and the boys came home from school, Slim was helping Heavy heat and dress the drill bit by hammering it with a sixteen-pound sledge.

"Can we climb to the top of the derrick, Slim?" shouted Orvie.

"You boys get out!" yelled Heavy crossly. "We're not gonna have a lot of mean little rowdy boys hangin' around this oil well."

"I was askin' *you*, Slim," shouted Orvie.

"NO!" yelled Slim. "YOU BOYS LISTEN TO HEAVY—HE'S BOSS HERE! It's too dangerous. Nobody's allowed up on the derrick except for business. Company rules. Now get out!"

"Want some pop?" yelled Orvie. "I'll go up to Peg-Leg's store and get you some."

"Sure, go ahead!" answered Slim, tossing out some coins.

Orvie rode off on his new bicycle. He rode it back and forth to school every day now to save time. Whenever he was at home, he left it near the well so the men could use it if they wanted to. Slim had told him that when they were taking time out, they liked to ride it up and down the road just for the fun of it.

When Orvie came back with the bottles of pop, the work on the drill bit was finished and Heavy was thirsty. He was more friendly now. He let Orvie and Harry Big Bear and Ralph Wilkins come into the doghouse and sit on the "lazy bench" and they all drank pop. Slim explained the danger of accidents from the heavy machinery, and the boys knew they must heed or be ordered off.

"Don't bump your head on the headache post!" laughed Slim, pointing to the post under the walking beam, as they came out on the derrick floor.

"Hi there, Slim! Hi there! Don't you hear me? *Slim! Slim!*"

They heard somebody calling Slim. Orvie looked over to the house and saw Della on the back porch. She called again, "Hi there, Slim! *Do you like rabbit?*"

"Yes, sure!" Slim called back.

"*Ain't the gravy good?*" shouted Della.

That was all. She switched around and went back into the house.

"Haw, haw, haw!" roared the tool-dresser. "If that girl don't take the cake!" Heavy and the boys laughed too.

"I'm not going to be a teamster or a rig-builder," Orvie an-

[53]

nounced to Grandpa that night. "I'm going to be a tool-dresser like Slim Rogers."

"Don't surprise me none!" said Grandpa with a smile.

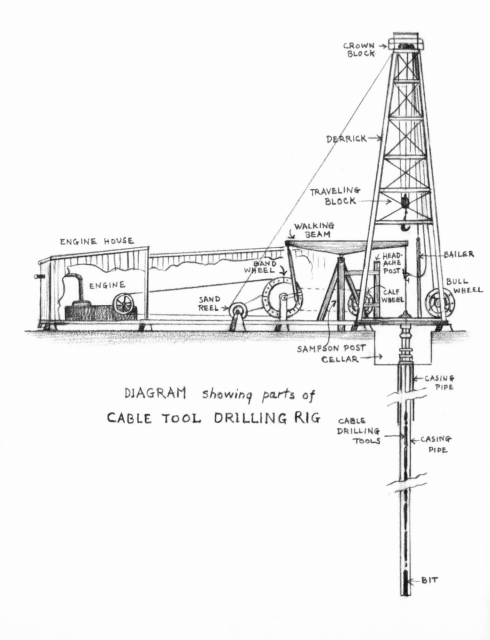

DIAGRAM showing parts of
CABLE TOOL DRILLING RIG

CHAPTER V

Stringtown

"DELLA, do wash Addie's face and comb her hair," said Mama one morning. "Her hair looks like a straw stack."

"Ain't been combed since Monday," mumbled Addie.

"Land sakes, and here it's Saturday," said Mama. "The days go by so fast I can't keep up with them. How long since you washed your face?"

"'Bout two weeks, Mama," said Addie, laughing.

The house was full of strangers. Orvie and Addie felt like strangers themselves. Mama was so busy she had no time for them. The change began one day when two oil workers came to the door and asked for a bed to sleep in. Papa and Mama talked it over.

"I don't want to take in roomers," said Mama, "but it seems

like I have to. There's no other place for the poor men to go. There's no place for 'em to eat, either, so they want me to let them eat with us."

"They make good wages, and they'll pay well," said Papa. "It's up to you."

Mama put the first two men into the spare room, and when the next two came, she moved Orvie and Bert into the attic and gave the men the boys' room. The rest of the family gave up their beds one by one. Mama slept on the leather couch and Papa on the floor of the front room. Della and Addie slept on beds made up on the dining room floor each night. When Mama put two men into the attic, Bert went out to the barn and Orvie moved to the porch swing. Only Grandpa remained comfortable and undisturbed out in his hen-house under the cottonwood tree.

One day a knock came at the door and Grandpa answered it.

"It's the 'farm boss' of the Sooner Oil Company, Jennie," he said. "He wants to arrange for a strip of land along the road, where people can build houses."

"They'll build houses?" asked Mama.

"Yes, a whole string of 'em," said Grandpa.

"Who'll live in them?" asked Mama.

"Oil workers and their families," said Grandpa. "They're nice folks. With oil wells springin' up like mushrooms, all the workers have to have places to live. It's too far for them to drive back and forth to Perry or Tonkawa every day. Do you want to be bothered about takin' in the rents, Jennie? You can add it to your chicken and egg money."

"All right, if they won't bother us," said Mama.

And so Stringtown—one of many Stringtowns—was built in

a week on the half-mile frontage of Robinsons' quarter-section. Lumber was hauled in over night and building began. Houses were moved in too, whole and readymade, blocked up in place and occupied immediately. People came in wagons, buggies and automobiles, bringing furniture. Before the end of the week, the Robinsons had many new neighbors.

At first Mama tried to see that she rented only to nice people, good people. But they came so fast she could not keep track of them all, and soon she was too tired to ask questions. If they said they would pay the rent, she told them to move in. She tried to remember their names—Armstrong, Cassady, Decker, Soaper . . .

"Can these people get water here, Mama?" asked Orvie.

"I suppose so," said Mama. "There's no other place. You help them pump, Orvie."

A procession of strangers—men, women and children—lined up at the well in the Robinsons' back yard with milk cans, pails, pitchers and bottles. Orvie pumped a while at first, and then gave up. The pump was always going. The people kept coming to the house, always wanting something. Mama began to sell them eggs, milk and cream, vegetables and chickens.

Mama was so busy she never noticed that Orvie had stopped school. He brought his books home one day and put them in the closet in his old room. He had decided not to go back, but he did not announce this to the family. He told them the latest oil news instead.

"They're spuddin'-in No. 2 back of the barn," said Orvie, "right in the puddle where the doodlebug wiggled!"

No. 2 Robinson had been staked off some time before, cellar

dug and rig erected. Wells had been started by half-a-dozen companies on neighboring farms. A few had proved to be dry holes, but there were more and more producers, so the field was considered proved territory.

"Oh, my land, I'll go crazy with two wells drillin' as close as that," said Mama. "No sleep at night and headache all day with all the racket goin' on."

"Slim's down to the Bartlesville sand in No. 1," Orvie went on, "and he's goin' on down to the Mississippi," Orvie explained. "They say there's seven sands and oil in every one of them—three of 'em for sure, and there's gonna be three derricks on every location."

"Seven sands!" Mama picked up the broom and began sweeping briskly. "Looks like I got seven sands right here in my house, what with all you menfolks keep trackin' in. Orvie, take hold of that wash-machine handle and get it goin'."

"Beds, beds, beds! I'm sick of makin' beds," complained Della.

"Hurry and bring the dirty sheets down, so I can put them in the machine," said Mama. "I got to get these pies and cakes in the oven, and the meat on to stew. The men ain't particular, but they like to eat hearty. I want 'em to have all they can hold."

"You feed 'em too good, Jennie," said Grandpa. "You won't make any profit on this deal."

"It does me good to see 'em eat," said Mama. "I never thought they'd be so nice. That Jenks feller—he's just a roustabout—brought me a present, a pretty silk handkerchief, yesterday. Of course I laid down the law to 'em when they first come. I told 'em they could play cards but no gambling or drinking in my house."

[58]

"They're good boys all right," said Grandpa. "That bunch on the Wilkins well got hijacked last night, robbed of every cent they had in their pockets—they'd just been paid off. There are always bad characters roamin' around, livin' off the gains of others."

"Orvie, what are you standing there gawkin' for?" cried Mama. "Take hold of the handle of that wash-machine. I must get those sheets out on the line before noon."

"Mama! Mama!" called Della from upstairs. "Somebody's knocking."

"Don't call so loud," answered Mama. "The night tour (tower) men must get their sleep." She put the cake into the oven and went to the door.

"Could I rent a room, Mrs. Robinson?" asked the well-dressed man who stood there.

"I'm full up as I can be," said Mama. "I could board you, but my beds are all full."

"My name's Jim Waterman," the man said, "I'm 'tool-pusher' for the Sooner Oil Company, in charge of all our wells around here. I have to see that they have supplies and equipment and keep going."

"That's *our* oil company, Mama," whispered Orvie.

"Could you give me a pillow and a quilt and let me sleep on the floor?" begged the man. "That would be better than the lazy-bench in the doghouse. Last night I had only my raincoat for a pillow, and the bench got mighty hard. All the boarding houses are full, with men sleeping in cots in the halls. They're sleeping in chairs in restaurants and barber shops, in parked cars —anywhere. So you see . . ."

[59]

"Why, that's terrible, and you a tool-pusher," said Mama. "But I haven't a place on earth to put you. There's somebody in every room but the kitchen, and I have to start the wood fire so early . . ."

"Mrs. Robinson, how would you like to have gas piped in to cook with? And for lights too?" asked Mr. Waterman. "You could cook quicker, and you wouldn't have to fill all those kerosene lamps. How would you like to have free gas?"

"Me? Free gas?" cried Mama. "I can't believe it."

"We'll pipe it in just as soon as we can," said Mr. Waterman. "Could you give me a pillow and quilt whenever I come and let me sleep here on the porch? I want to be as close to your oil well as possible. I won't be regular, I come and go, but when I come, I'll need a bed."

Mama laughed. "Why, of course, Mr. Waterman, if you don't mind Orvie in the porch swing. We'll buy you a cot and fix you up comfortable."

The next day was Sunday, but not the quiet peaceful Sunday of the past. The two Robinson wells were drilling away, shattering the Sunday peace with their loud commotion. The oil workers went about their work as usual, dressed in dirty everyday clothes. Mama and Della were so busy cooking all morning, nobody thought about going to church.

Della put all the extra leaves in the dining table, so it stretched from window to door. There were two sittings because Cousin Mattie and Cousin George, with their three grown-up children, came from Blackwell to spend the day, and Aunt Lottie and Uncle Mart dropped in on their way home from church. Orvie and Addie never got to sit down at all. They ran back and forth to the kitchen and helped themselves to dishes of food sitting there. They peeked through the crack of the door and listened to the conversation.

"They say they're going to drill in the cemetery, right by the Prairie View Church!" announced Aunt Lottie briskly.

"Goodness gracious!" exclaimed Cousin Mattie. "Can't they let the dead alone?"

"Jennie, do you hear?" called Lottie. "They won't even let the dead lay in peace."

But Mama was out in the kitchen cutting pie.

"Likely the oil field runs in that direction," said Uncle Mart. "They say it runs from southwest to northeast and then swings over west again. Likely it runs right in under the cemetery."

"There's always oil under a graveyard, they say," put in Cousin Mattie.

"Sandy Watkins won't let them drill there," said Papa. "He gave that land for the church and cemetery. His folks are buried there."

After the meal was over, Orvie walked out of the house with Shep at his heels. The novelty of the oil wells had worn off. The drilling seemed endless, and as long as it continued, there was no excitement. Orvie felt like his father. They were drilling clear down to China and not finding oil.

He went slowly down the road past the row of little String-town houses which lined the ditch. They were the smallest houses he had seen in his life. They sat close together, with just enough space between to park a car. Some of the cars looked larger than the houses.

No one acted as if it were Sunday. A woman was washing

clothes in a wooden tub. Another was hanging bedding out to air. Strange children were playing about. Orvie wondered if he would ever get to know them, and which name belonged to which —Cassady, Armstrong, Decker . . .

Pounding and sawing were going on everywhere. A new house was going up—twelve feet wide, eight feet high and sixteen feet long. The walls were made of one thickness of boards, with window frames protruding on the outside. A two by twelve plank rested on its narrow edge, reaching from front to back of the building. A man was laying roof boards on, curving them over to give enough slope to shed water.

"This your house?" inquired Orvie.

"Gonna be," said the man. "We're fixin' to move in tomorrow. Laid the first timber this morning."

"Awful funny roof," remarked Orvie.

"Box-car roof," answered the man. "We call it a box-car house.

Quick to build and good enough to live in. We always have 'em in the oil fields. I'm Ed Soaper, roustabout."

The man's wife and children came and stared at Orvie.

"Gonna plaster inside?" asked Orvie. "You'll freeze to death in the wintertime with only thin boards for walls."

"No, bub," laughed the man. "Not when we git gas piped in."

"We'll git free gas and we'll roast ourselves to death," said the woman, laughing.

"My name's Charley," said the nine-year-old boy. "Charley Soaper. That's a nice dog you got. You live up there where we get water, don't you?"

Orvie nodded.

Ed Soaper glanced up the road. "Here comes somebody in too big a rush to build him a house. He's movin' one in."

Orvie hurried up to watch. Several teams of horses were pulling a one-room house with rollers under it. Two men followed behind, picked up the rollers and ran to the front to put them under again. The house made slow progress.

"Want a ride?" called the driver, when they came to the corner.

"Sure," said Orvie. He looked at the sign in big letters above the front door. OSAGE TORPEDO HOUSE it said. He wondered what it meant, as he stepped inside and rode along.

The house was moved around the corner onto the side road. Here were more of the hastily-built shacks along the edge of Grandpa's wheat field. The house was set at the end of the line, near the alfalfa field.

"Who's going to live here?" asked Orvie.

"Them folks," said the driver. He pointed to a truck loaded

with people and furniture, which had driven up. A girl climbed down and sat on a box to watch the unloading. She was pretty and wore a flowered white dress and a straw hat. Orvie went over to talk to her.

"Are you going to live here?" he asked.

"Yes," said the girl.

"Your father . . ." began Orvie.

"He's a shooter," explained the girl.

"Oh!" said Orvie. He did not know what a shooter was. He looked at the sign over the door of the building. "What's that?" he asked.

"For dynamite," said the girl.

"Oh!" said Orvie again.

"It used to be for storage," the girl went on, "but now we're going to live in it. We couldn't find any other place."

"Oh!" said Orvie. "My name's Orville Robinson. What's yours?"

"Bonnie Jean Barnes," said the girl.

"I . . . I had a ride in your house," said Orvie.

But the woman called and the girl went into the Osage Torpedo House. Orvie wondered how it would feel to live there.

He cut into the field and wandered slowly across the prairie. Shep scampered along happily. It was quiet out in the field. He was away from the noise of the oil wells and the noise of many people. The earth seemed to have flattened out and the sky was a blue dome overhead. The sun was hot on his back and a good stiff wind was blowing. It was just the kind of day that he liked.

Suddenly he saw Shep chasing a jackrabbit in the pasture ahead. A jackrabbit was larger than a cottontail, with very long

[64]

ears and much larger, stronger hind legs. The rabbit was wise—
it acted as if it were crippled and let the dog come close. Then
suddenly it ran off and hid behind a bush. Shep came up sniffing.
The rabbit kicked the dirt up in his face and was off again. Orvie
laughed as he saw the long-legged creature go flying up the slope,
its ears laid back, making jumps twenty feet in length. What
chance did poor Shep have?

Orvie decided it was time to go for the cows, so he went to
the barn and climbed on Star's back. Dusk was gathering as he
headed for Cottonwood creek. In warm weather the cows sought
the thickest brush to get relief from flies and ticks. It was hard
to hunt them out, one by one, from the dense plum and black-
berry bushes, overgrown with wild grapevines.

Orvie wondered where they were tonight. So much had happened, he had not been to the creek lately. Bert had been bringing the cows in. To his surprise he saw lights flickering among
the bushes. He slapped Star's back and trotted over. Shep came
running behind.

The creek was greatly changed. He hardly knew it.

In among the shady trees and bushes, homeless campers lived
in tents or makeshift huts. They were "hangers-on"—people who
followed the oil booms, hoping to get jobs or money by fair or
unfair means. Some of them were ragged, others wore few
clothes. It had been a very hot day and the air had not yet cooled
off. Orvie could see beds inside the tents and people lolling on
them. He saw smoky campfires and women trying to cook.
Ragged, barefoot children were breaking branches off the trees
and throwing them on the fires. Others were sliding down the
dirt banks of the deep gully or wading in the creek.

Orvie slid off Star's back and let her stand. Shep came close.

"Where you folks from?" Orvie demanded, approaching a blowsy, fat woman, who held a greasy skillet over a fire. "This is my Grandpa's farm. Did he say you could camp here?"

The woman laughed a loud, coarse laugh, which made Shep growl. Orvie pulled the dog back. The woman called to a group of men sitting on the ground behind a tent, playing a game. They had bottles in their hands.

The men called back to the woman in words that Orvie did not understand. They tipped their bottles and drank. They threw the empty bottles in Orvie's direction.

"Git along home to your rich old Grandpa!" cried the woman. They were all looking at him now.

The ragged children dashed forward and threw stones at Orvie and the dog. As he turned away, Orvie noticed that the grass was strewn with empty bottles. He stumbled and fell. The next minute an overgrown boy was on his back, pounding him hard. But Shep set up a wild barking, then began to nip the boy's heels. The boy jumped off and backed away, afraid.

Orvie ran across the pasture to catch Star, who had started to run. Then he had to stop and sit down for a while. He felt so sick he was afraid he might lose his dinner. Shep came up and lay down beside him, panting. He patted the dog on the back.

Orvie felt sick in another way, too. The creek, where he had had such happy times wading and fishing, was spoiled. It was spoiled for him forever. He must keep Addie away. She must not see the creek the way it was now. Addie was too little to understand such things.

Orvie rode the pony slowly back across the fields to the farm-house. The farmhouse too had changed so he hardly knew it. It did not seem like home any more.

Before he reached the barn lot, before he could hear the noise and vibration of the two oil wells, he stopped suddenly for a strange sound struck his ear. It was music—loud, noisy music, the kind of music that kept on getting louder and louder as if it would never stop. Then it stopped for a minute, quieted down, but soon began all over again.

Orvie listened to see which direction it was coming from. All at once he knew. It was coming from the Pickerings' farmhouse down the road. He remembered Mrs. Pickering's visit on the day of the hailstorm. Old Pickering had done just what she said he would do. He had started a filling station across from Moore's store and he and his wife were living upstairs. The old farm-house, one of the first built after the Run, had been turned into a dance hall. That was where the music was coming from.

Orvie put Star in the barn and started for the house. He must tell Bert to go after the cows.

He walked over to the oil well at the side of the house. Just then its lights came on. The derricks were lighted up with elec-tric lights from bottom to top at night, so the night tour could continue the drilling.

Orvie felt sick again.

Even night was changed to day.

CHAPTER VI

Boom Town

"HERE's a nickel for you to spend, Addie," said Papa. "And a nickel for you, Orvie."

"Thank you, Papa." Orvie took a good look at the coin before he put it in his pocket. He thought of things he might buy with it.

After a rainy week, it was threatening rain again, but the family decided to go to Tonkawa anyway. It was several weeks since they had been there and various things were needed.

"I must get a new teakettle," said Mama. "My old one has sprung a leak."

"Can I get me a new summer hat?" asked Della.

"That bay team needs new harness," said Papa.

"I want to look at tractors," said Bert.

"All I want is a couple o' plugs of chewing tobacco," said Grandpa.

A trip to town on Saturday was always a great event, the high spot of the whole week. Everybody hurried to get ready. Mama and the girls put on fresh clothes, and the boys wore coats and caps.

The road was soft from the rains and the ruts were deep. Papa drove the Ford slowly and carefully. The family talked sociably as they rode along. Orvie took his nickel out of his pocket now and then to look at it.

Mama stared at the row of little houses that lined Grandpa's farm.

"I never knew there were so many," she said. "And what's that? A circus right here at the crossroads? What's that big tent for?"

"It says BUNKS on the front," said Papa. "Must be a place for men to sleep."

"We're gittin' a town right out here in the country—a boom town!" chuckled Grandpa. "It reminds me of Perry, on the night of the Cherokee Run, way back in 1893. Perry grew into a town over night—a tent town."

"Gosh almighty, just look!" exclaimed Papa. "Last week these stores weren't here. Now look at 'em, there's a café, a shoe shop, machine and blacksmith shops . . ."

"A barber shop," said Bert.

"And a drug store," added Della.

"Bet that's Old Pickering's filling station," said Orvie, pointing.

"And all those shack-houses in between," said Mama. "Why,

[70]

there must be hundreds of people come to live here now. I had no idea . . . Look at the oil wells drillin' right close behind all the stores and makin' all that racket."

Orvie had been reading signs stuck up on buildings or telephone poles: TOM'S SHOE SHOP, BUCKING HORSE CAFÉ, Ambulance phone 473, O. K. FEED STORE, LONG HORN MEATS, Doc McGuire call 95, POOR BOYS CAFE, Ironing Done 2 doors South, THE GUSHER drinks & everything, SUNFLOWER DRY GOODS, I Do Sewing, Hot Cakes & Donuts . . .

"Don't know if we'll ever get to Tonkawa," mumbled Papa. He was having a hard time keeping in the road, there were so many cars and wagons churning up the mud. The big wagon in front of the Robinson Ford slowed up. The line of vehicles ahead of it had stopped. Those going south were straddling deep ruts, or slipping down into the soft ditch. A horse pulling a mud-boat was carrying people across to the other side.

"We should have stayed at home when the road's as slick as this," said Mama. "We'll stick sure."

The Ford stopped with a jerk. Papa got out and walked ahead to see what the trouble was.

A boy on the board sidewalk called out, "Where you goin', Orvie?" He came up to the car, and they all saw that he had red hair and freckles.

"To Tonkawa, if we can ever get there," answered Orvie.

"Who is this boy?" asked Mama.

"Freckles, we call him. He's a new boy in my class at school, Mama," Orvie explained. "His father, Ed Hart, runs that place there—the Bucking Horse Café. Don't he, Freckles?"

[71]

"Yes," said Freckles proudly. "See that bucking horse on the front window—a cowboy painted it. It brings in lots of customers."

Papa came back. "They say Birds Nest Creek is bank full and so is Salt Fork River. The water's over the road, so we can't get through to Tonkawa. And up front, by that filling station, there's a chug hole big enough to drownd a horse in. A feller will pull you through with a tractor for five dollars. Guess who it is."

"I haven't an idea," said Mama.

"Old Pickering!" sputtered Papa. "Ain't that just like him?"

Freckles spoke up. "He's pulled a hundred and forty-seven cars through already. Do you know what he does every night? Digs the hole out deeper and hauls water in a barrel on a sled and dumps it in. I saw him!"

"Low-down skunk!" growled Grandpa. "Trust him to make even a mud-hole profitable. Always some people makin' profit out of others' misfortunes."

"Did you hear about that mule that dropped plumb out of sight yesterday?" asked Freckles.

"No, where?" inquired Orvie.

"Down in the mud, of course!" laughed Freckles. "I been doin' a good business sellin' drinkin' water, five cents a glass."

"You have?" said Orvie, astonished.

"Peg-Leg's pump is the only well water in town," the boy went on, "and people get thirsty, don't they? There's my stand." He pointed.

Grandpa frowned. "Young man, you takin' lessons from Old Pickering?" But Freckles did not answer. He hurried off down the sidewalk.

"You folks get out now and go in the stores here," said Papa. "I'll see if I can get turned around somehow."

Papa lifted Addie and Della out and carried them one at a time across the muddy road to the opposite side. He found some loose boards and put them down for Orvie, Mama and Grandpa to walk on.

"My land!" exclaimed Mama. "Where did all these people come from? Last week when I came to Peg-Leg's to do my trading, there was no town here at all."

"It's an over-night oil field," said Grandpa. "This is what you call a 'boom town.' Some of 'em gets built in three days, but our'n took a week."

The board sidewalk was crowded with people, operators, lease dealers, promoters, gamblers, oil workers, strangers of every kind. Real-estate men stood on boxes and shouted bargains. Hawkers peddled little bottles of oil for souvenirs, others sold maps. Men had desks on the boardwalk and were doing various kinds of business.

The Robinsons hardly recognized Moore's Store when they came to it, for other buildings hugged it now on both sides. The oil well behind it was hammering noisily and shaking the building with its vibration. Inside, the store was very crowded. Peg-Leg was beaming from ear to ear and running his wooden leg off, trying to wait on customers.

"I hear you folks are millionaires!" he called out to Grandpa.

"Not yet, but soon!" answered the old man gaily.

Orvie went up to the counter with Mama. Addie pressed her nose against the glass of the candy counter, and after parting with her nickel, began to chew on a mouthful of gumdrops. Orvie studied the sticks of black licorice. He didn't like the taste much, but it made saliva good and black, and when he spat it out, it looked like real tobacco juice.

Then he saw White Cloud, the old Otoe Indian, come in, as stolid-faced and mournful as ever.

"White Cloud, have you buried that baby yet?" Peg-Leg called out.

"*What* baby?" asked the Indian.

"The one you had to have money for the funeral for."

"Baby not dead yet," said White Cloud. "Got well plenty quick."

The people standing around laughed heartily. Mama and Della went to buy groceries in the back part of the store. Freckles Hart came in.

"See those men out there?" He pointed to a group of men, dressed in leather coats, leather-faced breeches, wearing high-laced, big-hole boots and carrying briefcases. "They're oil men —they always dress in leather."

He pointed again. "See that man there in front of my Pa's place?"

Orvie looked out and saw a man wearing a light cream-colored cowboy hat and cowboy boots with high heels.

"That's Two-Gun Jimmy," said Freckles. "He's deputy-sheriff. He shoots with two guns at the same time and never misses his mark. He eats at our place."

"Oh!" said Orvie, open-mouthed.

"There! He's gone in now to get his dinner."

The man disappeared inside the Café.

"See that man walkin' along there across the street?" Freckles went on. "That's Hooky Blair. He got his right hand blowed off in an explosion and he wears a hook."

"A *hook?*" exclaimed Orvie, staring at the man.

"Yes, an iron hook," said Freckles earnestly. "You can't see it, he's got it stuffed in his pocket. He eats with it and everything."

"Why don't he eat with his left hand?" asked Orvie.

"He uses his hook, I've seen him," said Freckles. "Hooky Blair and Two-Gun Jimmy are the two meanest men in town. They used to be outlaws and Hooky's been in the Pen, but they're law enforcement officers now. They arrest the oil field workers when they drink too much. There's a driller called the Chief. Hooky beat him up once. Then he ordered him out of town and told him if he ever came back he would kill him. You better not be hangin' around when them two gets to shootin'."

"No," said Orvie nervously. "I wouldn't want to be around."

"But I will," bragged Freckles, "and I'll tell you what happens. I've lived in oil fields all my life. Bet I've seen more men killed than you have."

Freckles went out and Orvie stared after him.

The crowd in the store got thicker and everybody was talking and laughing. There seemed to be unusual excitement. Then all at once, there was Peg-Leg calling to the people to listen. He mounted a chair, then stood on the counter and shouted:

"Friends, there's been more people in my store in the last two days than there ever was in a month of Sundays before. It used to be so quiet around here, you could hear a penny go *plop* when it rolled in the dust. I'm feelin' mighty good today . . ."

"Hooray!" shouted the crowd.

[77]

"Because they're pumpin' five hundred barrels of oil a day from the well right in back of my store," Peg-Leg went on.

"Hooray!" cried the people.

"I ain't just happy—I'm delirious! Whoopee!" Peg-Leg began to dance a little jig.

"Whoo-pee! Whoo--pe-e-e!" echoed the people.

"What you gonna do with all your money?" asked a voice from the crowd.

"I been figurin' and figurin'," said Peg-Leg, with a twinkle in his eye. "I've wore my wooden leg down two inches waitin' on so many customers this last week, I guess I'll splurge and buy me a factory-built wooden leg!"

"Whoo-pee! Whoo-pee!" yelled the crowd.

"And that ain't all," Peg-Leg went on. "We got a new town right here, that's growed up in a week, and I'm gonna give it a name. It's a boom town, an oil town, a get-rich-quick town! It come in with a whizz and it landed with a bang. Let's call it Whizzbang!"

"WHIZZBANG! O. K. Let's call it WHIZZBANG!" answered the people. "A good name for a town—WHIZZBANG!"

"And that ain't all," the storekeeper continued. "I'm so happy today, I'm givin' everybody here a present."

He reached down into his cash drawer with two hands and tossed out handfuls of loose change. Pennies, nickels, dimes, quarters, silver dollars and half-dollars flew through the air, bounced and rolled over the floor. The coins hit people in the face, landed in hands or pockets, or were jounced off shoulders in the scuffle that ensued. The next minute Peg-Leg's customers were down on their hands and knees, trying to gather free money into their pockets.

"Happiness has gone to my head!" cried the storekeeper. He laughed and laughed till tears came to his eyes, as he tossed handful after handful of loose change into the air.

"Look at 'em!" he cried, pointing. "Look at the greedy pigs—my customers." Then he began laughing again. Peg-Leg laughed until he could not stop.

After the people had gathered up all the coins from the floor, Peg-Leg was still laughing. A woman pounded him on the back, but he did not stop. A man threw a pailful of water in his face. The storekeeper gulped a few times, wiped his face on a bolt of silk from the counter, and stopped laughing. The crowd thinned out and went away, telling a new tale of Peg-Leg's fantastic riches.

All through the excitement, Orvie wondered where Mama was. He tried to pick up some of the coins, but had his hands and toes stepped on. He edged his way to the door and went outside. He had had enough of the money-mad crowd and he wanted to get way from it. He saw more people, all strangers, trying to shove and push into the store, as news of free money spread down the street.

Orvie found a place near the corner of the building, where he could watch through the show-window. The sight made him feel sick, so he turned away. In the road, cars and wagons were still churning the mud and making the chug-holes deeper. Orvie wished he were safe at home again.

At last Mama and Della and Addie came out of the store. Mama's hat was crooked, Della's hair was wild, and she had lost the tie to her middy. Addie was crying at the top of her voice.

"Thank goodness!" said Mama. "We thought you got knocked over and trampled on, Orvie. We couldn't see you anywhere. I called and you didn't answer. Are you all right?"

"Yes, Mama, I'm all right," said Orvie.

"Did you get any money?" asked Della.

"Naw—didn't want none," said Orvie. "Got a couple sore toes."

"I got a quarter and a silver dollar and a dime and a half-dollar," said Della, "a dollar and eighty-five cents all together."

"I got a quarter and two nickels," said Addie through her tears.

"Wasn't Peg-Leg a sight!" exclaimed Mama. "Everybody's so glad to see him come into all that money, and wasn't he generous? If he'd get sixteen wells, it wouldn't give him the big head. He'd still be the same old Peg-Leg."

'I want to spend my free money, Mama," said Della. "Let's go in this new Sunflower Dept. Store and look for my hat."

"Have you seen Papa yet, Orvie?" asked Mama.

"No," said Orvie.

"He'll come for us, once he gets the car turned around and is ready to go home," said Mama.

Mama and Della led the way, and Orvie and Addie followed.

The new store had a big counter full of fancy hats. A young, stylishly dressed woman, with light yellow hair and very pink cheeks was trying on a variety of hats. They all had wide, floppy brims, and plumes or red roses on them. Mama stared at her suspiciously.

"Is that the woman I rented that last little house to? The one in the alfalfa field?" Mama asked Della.

"It looks like her, Mama," said Della. "Hazel Daley she said her name was."

"Yes, that's her," said Addie. "She came to the pump for water this morning and she called me 'dearie'."

"What makes her cheeks so pink?" whispered Della.

"That's red paint on 'em," said Mama. "She's a wicked woman. Where'll she ever wear a hat with a long plume like that in this town?"

"It'll be her Sunday hat," said Della. "I think it's awful pretty. She'll wear it to the Prairie View church. Do you think I have enough money to buy one like it?"

"To church?" sniffed Mama. "That kind of a woman never puts her nose inside a church."

"Why, Mama, she's pretty and . . ."

"Did you hear the price of that hat?" asked Mama. "Twenty dollars, but the clerk said she could have it by paying two-fifty down. Come, let's get out of here."

"But Mama, my new hat . . ." wailed Della.

"Your little dollar eighty-five won't go very far in a place like this." Mama marched the children out of the door.

Bert came back to the car disgusted—he had seen no tractors at all, only oil machinery. Papa had no new harness and Mama hadn't found a teakettle. Della had no new hat and Addie's gum-drops were gone. Only Grandpa was happy, vigorously chewing tobacco. Orvie wished he had bought his licorice, so he could spit too.

On the way home the Ford slid and skidded over the wet clay road. The Robinsons became alarmed by heavy clouds of black smoke which they saw curling up ahead. The unpleasant stench of burning oil and gas fumes filled the air.

"An oil well's caught fire," said Papa, "or else a slush-pond's on fire somewhere."

"Hope it's not ours," said Mama nervously.

"No, it looks too far to the east," said Grandpa.

The fields were all filled with oil derricks, and the old farm landscape had disappeared. A new and strange oil field had taken its place. There was no longer the green of growing wheat or grass pasture to be seen, but black oil everywhere, spreading out to kill growing plants and to devastate the face of the earth. It was a wonder the fires did not occur more often.

When the Robinsons reached home, they could see that the oil fire was more than a mile away, in the section east of the old Pickering place. Many cars were heading in that direction, clogging the muddy roads.

"Orvie, go see if everything's all right out at our slush-pond," said Mama, "and chase those cows away. They seem bound to get at that salt water. They are after the salt, but the oil will kill them. We've lost four cows already and we can't afford to lose more."

"Can't we?" chuckled Grandpa.

"I won't stand by and see my cows kill themselves," said Mama. "I've always liked cows."

Orvie started for the pasture. He picked up a stick and chased the cows. Grandpa followed with Shep.

"Papa will have to build a fence around the slush-pond," said Orvie. "We can't be forever chasin' cows."

"The oil company ought to do that for us," said Grandpa.

"Grandpa," said Orvie, "wouldn't it be nice to climb to the

[84]

top of the derrick some time? Harry wants to and so does Ralph."

"Slim told you boys to stay off," said Grandpa.

"I'd like to tell Freckles Hart what it feels like to be up so high," Orvie went on. "He's always braggin' about all the men he saw get killed. I bet I could see over the top of the world, if I got up on that catwalk on top. I bet I'd feel like I could fly faster'n a bird."

"Mebbe so," said Grandpa. "Wouldn't surprise me none."

Suddenly a loud roaring filled the air. Grandpa and Orvie looked up in the sky, and saw an airplane come closer and closer. It seemed to be circling round the Robinson farm.

"Golly, Grandpa, look! It's coming *here!*"

The airplane circled, banked and came slowly down. It landed in the level wheat field behind the barn. Orvie and Grandpa ran over just as three men stepped out. They were dressed in leather coats and wore high-laced boots, so Orvie knew they were oil men. Then he recognized Jim Waterman, the tool-pusher.

"So much high water between here and Ponca City," Waterman explained, "we decided to fly over."

"When it rains around here, it just won't quit," said Grandpa.

"Bad fire over east here," said Waterman. "We'll get a car to take us over." He looked down at Orvie, then pointed to the airplane. "Would you like a ride, son?"

"A ride?" Orvie could not believe his ears. "In the plane?"

Grandpa spoke up. "I'm afraid his folks wouldn't let him go up in an airplane . . ."

Orvie's face fell. "Aw, Grandpa, they wouldn't care."

"Unless some responsible member of the family went along!" added Grandpa, laughing. "Orvie and me's ready any time, Mr.

Waterman. We was just sayin' we wished we could see over the top of the world or else fly like a bird."

Mr. Waterman spoke to the pilots. "Take these two passengers up for a fifteen minute flight. Then come back and wait for us. We'll start back to Ponca in an hour." He walked away with the oil men.

The ride was more wonderful than Orvie had ever dreamed it could be. He was still up in the clouds when he came down again. He put his hand in his pocket. There was Papa's nickel—it brought him back to earth.

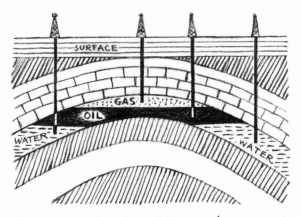

DIAGRAM showing OIL underground

CHAPTER VII

No. 1 Robinson

ORVIE sat on the grass under the cottonwood tree, fixing his
bicycle. He had it all apart, and the parts were scattered
around. The long clothesline around the corner of the house
was full of bedding."

"Here, boy, come and pump for me." A woman stood by the
pump with two bottles in her hands.

Orvie jumped up and began to pump. The woman was Hazel
Daley, whom they had seen in the Sunflower Dept. Store. She
said that her husband was Jack Daley, a driller, and he made
high wages, ten dollars a day. Hazel was young and pretty—
Orvie liked pumping for her.

Other women came to the well, carrying pails, pans and buckets, and bringing their children. Mrs. Barnes came, pulling a
sled with two large milk cans on it, but Bonnie Jean was not
with her.

"Why don't you bring something bigger?" Orvie asked Hazel
Daley.

"I haven't any cooking pots or buckets," she answered.

"How do you cook then?" inquired Mrs. Soaper. Her small
girl and boy were hanging to her skirts, while Charley carried
her buckets.

"I don't!" Hazel Daley laughed. "We eat at the Bucking Horse
Café. I haven't any dishes either. But I can make coffee and open
tin cans."

The women looked at each other with raised eyebrows.

"Have you heard the news?" asked Hazel. "A man was killed last night . . ."

"Where?" gasped Orvie.

"Up on Pistol Hill," said Hazel. "The sheriff got there too late. The killer got away." She took her bottles and disappeared around the corner of the house.

When she was gone, Mrs. Armstrong said, "She bought another swell hat."

"Another?" cried Mrs. Decker. "Bet it ain't paid for."

"I live in the house right next door to the Daleys," said Mrs. Barnes. "That woman and her husband fought and screamed all last night. We couldn't get any sleep."

"They must have been drinking," said Mrs. Cassady.

"There's a bootlegger got a still down by Cottonwood creek," said Mrs. Soaper. "They don't have to go far for it. Notice them *jugs* she carried?"

"A bootlegger—what's that?" piped up Orvie.

"Don't *you* know?" Mrs. Soaper's boy, Charley, let his mother pump her buckets full and came over to talk to Orvie.

"It's a man who makes liquor," Charley went on, "and charges plenty for it. His name is Nicky Grimes and he needs empty whisky bottles. I know where we can find some. Would you like to make a little easy money?"

Orvie remembered the nickel in his pocket and how seldom Papa handed nickels out. "Yes, I would," he said.

"Come with me, then," said Charley.

The two boys started off toward the barn, where they stopped to pick up a tow sack.

"You've got a pony, ain't you?" asked Charley.

Orvie nodded. They mounted Star and rode off over the pasture.

The women and children went back to their box-car houses

and Mama was kept so busy, she did not miss Orvie at all. A string of salesmen kept knocking at the door. They tried to sell Mama everything from automobiles and pianos and organs, to radios, phonographs and wash-machines. To all of the men, Mama said: "We haven't struck oil yet."

One salesman was hard to get rid of. He had a large Silvertone Cabinet Model radio. "Quite a lot of producers in this neighborhood," he argued. "You'll strike oil any day now."

"Can I get a piano and take music lessons?" begged Della.

"I don't sell pianos," snapped the salesman.

"I got talked into making a payment on a gas stove that I can't use because we have no gas," said Mama. "Oh yes, they're going to pipe it in, but they haven't done it yet."

"You can use this radio even if you have no electricity," said the man. "It's a seven-tube Silvertone battery-operated receiver with dynamic speaker. Now for the first time you can enjoy musical and voice reproduction with lifelike fidelity. Cash price only ninety-eight dollars, or thirty days trial and nine-fifty a month . . ."

"There comes the truck with my new stove now." Mama left the salesman, who got discouraged and went away. She told the truck man to put the stove on the back porch. "I'll never use it anyway. Orvie, chop up some wood and fill the woodbox."

Orvie had just come back, overheated and breathless. While the oil workers were eating dinner, Mama stirred up her daily batch of bread. Another knock came at the front door.

"Tell that salesman to go away, Della," called Mama.

But it was not a salesman. "He's Superintendent of the Tumbleweed Oil Company, and he wanted to see Papa, but says you'll do, Mama."

Mama turned the bread dough over to Della and went in.

"Your husband is on the Cemetery Committee of the Prairie View church, I understand, Mrs. Robinson," the man began.

"Oh," said Mama. "Now I know what you're after. Yes, Al's on the Committee, but we wouldn't think of consenting to let *any* oil company drill in the churchyard or cemetery."

"But lady," said the Superintendent, "think of all you'll be losing. We'll make the congregation rich. You have let oil wells come right here in your dooryard . . ."

"Yes sir," said Mama, "and many's the time I've regretted it, but we needed the money so bad. Farming's a hard way to make a living."

"Now in the cemetery . . ." began the Superintendent.

"Would the derrick be higher than the church steeple?" Orvie asked.

"Just about twice as high, son," said the man, smiling.

"You hush up, Orvie," scolded Mama. "We'll never give our consent. Even if the men will, the women won't. Something's got to be kept sacred. You're ruining our homes and our farms, and still you're not satisfied. My baby daughter lies buried in that cemetery."

"But lady, we'll dig ditches and drain the oil and salt water off . . ."

Mama couldn't say another word. She went to the door, opened the screen and ushered the man out. Then she sank down in a rocker and buried her face in her hands.

Orvie looked on, distressed. "But Mama, he didn't say he was going to, he only asked if he *could*."

Mama did not look up. "My little baby . . . my little baby . . ." she kept on crying.

"Mama, just looky here what I got," cried Orvie, in an effort to cheer her. He reached in his pocket and pulled out a handful of coins.

"Orville Robinson!" Mama got up from her chair. "Where did you get all that money? Your Papa . . . no . . . Did Grandpa give you all that?"

"No, Mama," said Orville, beaming. "I earned it myself. I knew you'd be glad."

"How did you earn it?"

"Well, me and Charley . . ." It wasn't so easy to tell after all.

"Charley Soaper? You haven't been runnin' around with that Charley Soaper and gettin' into mischief?"

"No Mama," Orvie went on. "Me and Charley just rode Star down to the creek and we took a tow sack along and we picked up a whole sackful of empty bottles. The people down there didn't bother me none 'cause Charley was along, they *know* Charley—and we took 'em to a man who paid us money for 'em. I knew you'd like to have the creek cleaned up a little. Those campers are makin' such a mess down there, they throw paper and tin cans and bottles all over everywhere . . ."

"Bottles!" Mama stared hard at Orvie. "What kind of bottles are you talking about?"

"Well, er . . . just bottles," said Orvie. "I guess . . . maybe they're old whisky bottles . . ."

"Why, Orville Robinson!" exclaimed Mama. "Me the President of the W.C.T.U. and you sellin' whisky bottles!" She lowered her voice. "Who did you sell them to?"

"Nicky Grimes," confessed Orvie. "Charley took me to Nicky's house, he knows where he lives—it's not far from here. Nicky's odd, Mama, but he was awful friendly and he laughed a lot and he give us five cents apiece for the bottles. I split with Charley. Thirty bottles at five cents apiece come to a dollar fifty, so we each got seventy-five cents. Charley said Nicky is called a boot . . . a bootlegger . . . that was it."

"Give me that money, Orvie," said Mama.

Orvie put the coins in Mama's outstretched hand.

"I hate to even touch it," she said.

"I can't have it—to spend?" asked Orville.

"No," said Mama. "Do you know what a bootlegger is and what he does?"

"No Mama," said Orvie.

"He makes strong drink secretly," said Mama. "Oklahoma's a dry state and it's against the law to make and sell it. So he breaks the law when he makes it. He'll put it in those bottles you

took to him and sell it to people secretly, and they'll drink it and get drunk. Drinking and drunkenness ruin people's lives and cause nothing but unhappiness. Did you know that?"

"No Mama," said Orvie.

"Well, you know it now and I don't want you to forget it."

"I won't do it again, Mama. But can't I have even a nickel of the money?" begged Orvie.

"No," said Mama. "We'll put it in the collection plate on Sunday. That way we'll know it will do a little good."

Just then Grandpa came in and Mama told him what had happened.

"Don't surprise me none," said the old man.

"Grandpa, Charley took me over to Pistol Hill and showed me where a man was killed last night," said Orvie. "Did you ever see a man get killed?"

"Oh, how can I raise my boys in a place like this?" cried Mama. "All this meanness and cuttin' up and even killin' going on on all sides . . ." She began to cry again.

Grandpa put his arm around her shoulder.

"The boy's got a lot to learn, Jennie," he said to Mama. "He'll learn it a little faster since oil's brought it so close to us, but it won't harm him none. Orvie's made of good stuff. He might as well learn young that there are all kinds of people in the world, evil as well as good."

Mama hurried out to the kitchen, saw that Della had put the loaves of bread into the oven, and was washing the dinner dishes. "I must bring that bedding in and make up the beds," she said, going out into the yard. In a moment she was back, visibly upset.

"Good land, what next! Two quilts are gone. That blue check

from Orvie's bed and your pink flowered one, Della—they're *gone.*"

"Gone?" echoed Della and Orvie. "Where could they go to?"

"Somebody took them. We're living in a nest of thieves. I hung those two quilts on the line this morning," said Mama, "and now they're gone."

"With all these strangers coming into the yard," said Della, "what can you expect?"

Mama went upstairs to make the beds, then went outside to look for the quilts again. She was in the side yard when Mr. Waterman appeared. Mama promised to get his cot made up, but did not notice how excited he was, or understand what he meant when he said he might not sleep in it after all. Mama was tired that night and went to bed early, so she did not know till the next morning that the men and boys never went to bed at all.

Orvie slept doubled up on the porch swing, wrapped in a comfort. He heard Mr. Waterman come up on the porch, sit on the cot for a while, then get up. Orvie threw off his comfort and followed. There was no moon and the oil well with its bright lights looked like a wonderful Christmas tree shining in the darkness. They sat up all night in the doghouse, and even Orvie did not get sleepy because something was expected to happen every minute. But it didn't.

Everybody talked excitedly the next morning, and the men and boys went back to the well right after breakfast. Mama caught two hens, chopped their heads off and scalded them. She was out behind the house, picking feathers off the second hen, when No. I Robinson blew in. Mama stood still and looked when she heard the loud explosion.

[95]

Gas came first, smothering the derrick in a white cloud of fumes. Then a fountain of thick black crude oil spouted up from the deep hole it had taken three long months to drill. It spouted high into the air, and a shower of oil and rocks peppered the Robinson house on the north.

Mama ran over to where all the people were standing. Della and Addie came along too.

"When do I get my new silk dress, Mama?" cried Addie, remembering how she had wished the well in so long ago.

"Better stand up wind," yelled Grandpa, "so you won't get covered with oil."

Orvie hurried over to Mama. "The bailer got thrown to the top of the derrick!" he shouted.

"The bailer? What's that?" asked Mama.

"It's a long bucket thing that they bail sand and mud out with," said Orvie. "When they see oil in it, they know she's comin', and oh boy! How she did come!"

People began to arrive from all directions. They came afoot, in wagons, buggies and cars. Big cars with town people, Fords and wagons with country people, everybody came to see the excitement. People stood about, talking, pointing and laughing. They kept coming all day long.

Orvie was so excited and happy, he felt as if he would burst. So much was happening, he just stood and watched.

He saw men throwing their hats up in the air. He saw Grandpa with a bottle of oil in his hands, walking about in puddles of oil, spoiling his shoes. He saw an oil man, dressed in leather, dance about and yell at the top of his voice, then bend over and wash his hands and face in oil, while the people shouted and laughed.

[98]

He saw Jim Waterman rushing about, telling men not to smoke or light a match, because of the fire hazard from the escaped gas. He saw Slim Rogers, covered with oil from head to toe, a broad smile breaking through his oil-stained face, wave a greasy hand to Della. He saw Mama crying and wondered what she was crying for.

Then Bert came up from the barn. Bert stood with his hands in his pockets, glaring at the derrick. Orvie ran over to him.

"Golly! Ain't you glad, Bert?" he asked. "Now you can get a new tractor."

Bert turned on him angrily. "You little fool, what do I want with a tractor—now that the farm's ruined?"

"What? You're not glad?" Orvie pranced about. "Betcha we'll be rich now. Betcha Papa'll give me a nickel to spend every week without me even askin' him."

Bert turned and went back to the barn.

People kept on coming. The road was crowded with cars, smashing each other's fenders and locking bumpers. They were racing to see who could get there first. Strangers came in and filled the yard, acting as if they owned the well themselves.

People crowded around the Robinsons and kept asking: "What are you going to do with all your money?" The Stringtown people and the campers from the creek joined the crowd. People never friendly before became close friends in a minute. Walt Pickering put one arm around Papa and the other around Grandpa. "Ain't it wonderful? Ain't it wonderful?" he shouted.

The people asked Papa to say something. He turned a large wash-tub over and stood on it. "Folks," he said "this has happened so all-fired sudden, we're not used to it yet . . . but I guess we'll buy us a new car . . . before our old Ford falls to pieces . . ."

Mama dried her eyes, got up on the tub and added: "And then we'll move to town!"

"What you gonna do with that chicken?" called a voice from the crowd.

Mama looked down and was surprised to see that she still held the half-plucked hen in her hand.

"Stew it for supper!" she cried, laughing.

"Hooray! Hooray!"

Then Grandpa took the tub. "Friends, this is the happiest day of my life," he said. "I've known for thirty years there was oil under this farm—that's why I've hung onto it through thick and thin. When the drillers talked about quittin', I says, 'You're not quittin' now. You suckers go ahead and drill a little deeper and you'll get it.' They drilled down a little ways, got to the bottom of that sand—and there she was, and here she is now, spoutin' out over the top! We're all gonna have things a little easier now. Too much hard work ain't good for nobody. It sure is great to be RICH!"

After a while Slim hurried over to Mama and Della and Addie.

"When do I get my new silk dress, Slim?" demanded the little girl.

"Tomorrow!" answered Slim. "You sure wished hard, Addie, to bring all this oil!"

"Just look what you did to our house, Slim," scolded Mama. "The whole side and all the windows covered with oil."

"We can't see out of a single window, Slim," added Della, laughing. "What do you mean, makin' me all that extra work?"

[100]

"Just as soon as I get this gusher under control," laughed Slim, "I'll come over and help you wash windows."

"Oh, will you, Slim?" cried Della. "Just look at your clothes. How are you ever going to get all that oil out of them?"

"Oh, I'll blow 'em out," said Slim. "We got the steam piped into a box-doin's over there by the doghouse. We put our greasy clothes in there and let 'em steam, then hang 'em on the fence . . ."

"I'll hang 'em on the clothesline for you, Slim," said Della. But Slim had hurried back to his work.

After everybody was gone, Orvie sat down in the little house under the cottonwood tree to talk to Grandpa. His face was still beaming with joy.

"I knew it was coming," he said. "Slim told me three weeks ago. Even when it didn't come all last night, I still knew it was coming."

"I've known it for thirty years," said Grandpa quietly.

"I'm glad I've already quit school," said Orvie.

"Quit school?" inquired Grandpa.

"Yes," said Orvie. "Three weeks ago when Slim first told me, I brought my books home. I'm not going back."

"Why not?"

"Well, you see the only thing an education is good for is to help a man get a living," said Orvie. "Now that we've struck oil, we'll be rich and I won't have to work for a living. So I don't need to go to school any more."

"Gonna sit around all your life and twiddle your thumbs, boy?"

Orvie laughed.

"Have you told your Mama?" asked Grandpa.

"No," said Orvie. "There's no need to mention it. You won't tell her, will you?"

"No," said Grandpa. The old man had not the heart to mar the boy's perfect happiness. He knew how rarely such happiness came in a lifetime.

"She'll find out soon enough," said Orvie.

"She sure will," said Grandpa.

CHAPTER VIII

The Milk Route

MAMA did find out soon enough. After a few days, when the excitement had died down, she asked Orvie, "Why aren't you in school?"

Orvie tried to tell her what he had told Grandpa, but Mama would not listen. "You get off to school now or I'll box your ears good," she said. "Bring your books home every night, to make up what you've missed."

"But there's no place to do homework," wailed Orvie. "The house is all filled with people sleeping everywhere . . ."

"You can study in the kitchen," said Mama.

The sudden growth of the town of Whizzbang had doubled Bert's milk route. He had twice as many customers as before, and every day brought new ones from the increasing number of oil workers. He drove the Ford, and besides milk, carried eggs and dressed chickens to sell. He served the restaurants, boarding houses and cafés as well as private families.

Mama decided that Orvie should get his morning chores done earlier, so he could go on the milk route with Bert. He was to carry the bottles from the car to the houses, to save Bert time. The route was planned so that Bert could drop Orvie off near the school just before the last bell rang.

Wet weather and muddy roads continued through April, and Papa bought Knobby Tread tires which did not skid so much.

It was a wet morning the day that Orvie started back to school. The Ford made a number of stops at the row of box-car houses down around the corner. It was very early, and most of the people were not up yet. Orvie took six quarts of milk at a time in his wire basket, and ran from one house to the next. At the Osage Torpedo house, the people were stirring, and there on the door-step stood the girl who had told him her name was Bonnie Jean. Orvie remembered about the dynamite.

"They've built a nitro-glycerin storage house on our place, back in the field," he told her. "When they wash out the buckets, they go *boom-boom-boom*. It shakes our house all over."

"They blow 'em up," said Bonnie Jean, taking the milk bottle. "You better stay away from there—it's dangerous."

"Say—oh say . . ." Orvie hesitated. "You started in school yet?"

"Why yes," said Bonnie Jean. "I started the very next day after we moved here."

"You did? Will you be at school today?" asked Orvie.

"Sure," said Bonnie Jean.

Orvie ran back to the car. The Ford traveled over the oil field in the section north of the Robinson farm, now called the Watkins lease, and stopped at Company houses recently built there, then came to the business part of town. It reached Bascom's boarding house just as breakfast was being served. Two untidy girls were waiting on long tables filled with men just inside the door.

"Take the milk into the kitchen," said Bert, "then come back for these eggs and chickens that Biddy ordered. Don't get scared of the old woman—she won't bite you."

Orvie went in at the open door.

"Hi, bub! Who are you?" called one of the men.

"You're Bert's brother Orvie, I bet." Biddy came forward, all smiles.

She started to pat him on the head, but Orvie dodged. He couldn't help staring at her. She wore three different skirts with an apron on top, long pantaloons below, and a sagging slip-on sweater around her waist. She walked on crutches, dragging one foot.

"I got banged up in an automobile accident," she explained, "one time when I was hitch-hiking. They wanted to cut my foot off, but I wouldn't let 'em. I can still hop around."

The men laughed and began teasing her.

"Now Orvie, my boy, put that milk out in the kitchen."

Orvie ducked into the back part of the house, returned, and brought in the eggs and chickens.

"How's that pretty sister of yours?" called the men.

Then Orvie saw Slim Rogers. He hadn't known where he lived before. Slim got up and stopped him just inside the door. "I'm going to be working at No. 2 Robinson," he said. "Tell Della, won't you?"

"Sure will!" called the boy.

"Hurry up!" scolded Bert when Orvie got back to the car. "If you want to get to school on time, you mustn't stand and gass all day when you're deliverin' milk. That won't get us nowhere."

"That old Biddy Bascom, she's a sight!" growled Orvie.

On the road west from Cloverleaf Corners the Ford got stuck in a chug hole.

"Get out," ordered Bert, "and see if you can find any fence rails."

Orvie started up the road. The fences were all wire fences, but maybe Jess Woods would have some rails. He headed for the Woods farm.

A car came along and pulled up behind Bert's Ford. Two girls jumped out and came running along the road. Orvie waited till they caught up. They were Edna Belle and Nellie Jo Murray. They looked fatter than ever and wore big galoshes to keep off the mud. They looked scared and were breathless from running.

"What you runnin' so fast for?" demanded Orvie.

"Hooky Blair's comin' after us," cried Edna Belle.

"He'll hook us with his hook," added Nellie Jo.

"I don't see him," said Orvie, looking back to the two cars. "Where is he?"

"He got in a car and drove it up close behind us," said Edna Belle.

"He followed us all the way till he turned off," said Nellie Jo.

"If he turned off, you don't need to be scared," said Orvie. "Does your father drive you to school every day?"

"No—our brother Ben," said Edna Belle. "That's him in our car back of Bert."

"He couldn't get past Bert without rollin' in the ditch," said Nellie Jo.

Just then Jess Woods came out of his lane. "Cars havin' trouble up there?" he called.

"Stuck in the mud," said Orvie. "Got any fence rails?"

Seeing that Bert had the help of Ben Murray and Jess Woods, Orvie walked on to school. The Murray girls flew on ahead of him, still fearful. Orvie walked slowly, thinking how silly they were, wondering why the last bell did not ring.

The Prairie View schoolhouse sat on a rise of ground at the next four corners. When Orvie got there, he had two surprises. He saw a new oil well on the school ground, with a derrick going up by the windows. And he saw Miss Plumley, coming from the opposite direction across a low damp field, walking. She was late, and all the children ran to the corner to meet her.

Orvie stared at Miss Plumley, forgetting to say good morning. "Did you stick too?" he asked.

"Yes, Orvie!" laughed Miss Plumley. "I left my car and took a short cut across the field. Then I had to wade the creek."

She looked so funny all the children laughed, and she did not seem to mind. Her feet and legs were bare and white to her knees. In one hand she carried her shoes and stockings, and held up her long skirt. In the other she carried a big bunch of pink and white roses. She walked timidly, letting out squeals each time something sharp stuck her tender feet.

"*Teacher's going barefoot! Teacher's going barefoot!*" sing-songed the children.

"I'm late," puffed Miss Plumley. "I had to stop to pick the little stickers out of first one foot, then the other."

"Stickers! Teacher don't like stickers!" giggled the children.

"And Mrs. Gordon made me stop and admire her roses," Miss Plumley went on. "She gave me this bouquet, and the roses have stickers too!"

Laughing, the children tumbled pell-mell into the schoolhouse, and Miss Plumley seemed more of a human being than she had been before, just because the children had seen her bare feet. She washed them, and put on her shoes and stockings. Orvie rang the last bell and school began.

He sat down in his seat and looked out the window.

To think they had started an oil well in the schoolyard during his absence. If he had known that, he never would have missed. The rig was much higher than the building, and from where he sat, he could see the drillers working. Maybe he could climb to the top of this derrick some time. The drilling shook the building, and ever so often the steam engine let off a blast of steam.

Orvie looked around, and there sat Bonnie Jean Barnes in

front of him. There were many other new faces. Every seat was taken and some held two. He recognized certain Stringtown children, Freckles Hart and other boys from Whizzbang. School was suddenly exciting—but it was hard to keep his mind on his books.

"We're too crowded," said Miss Plumley," with so many new children, but we'll get along. Perhaps next year we'll have a new school building. We must try to get used to the drilling outside our windows and not pay too much attention to it. Now Orvie, you have a lot of work to make up . . ."

A swishing burst of steam drowned the sound of her voice, and the rest of Orvie's scolding for being absent could not be heard.

"We'll have to talk fast, then stop and take a breath while the noise lasts," Miss Plumley went on. The children laughed. "Orvie, will you please read the first paragraph of . . ."

Pz-z-z-z-z-t! Pz-z-z-z-z-t! sizzled the steam again.

And so it went all day long. Each time they started something, the bursts of steam stopped them. Miss Plumley had to give in-structions by signs because of the noise. The vibration shook the building. Desks and furniture shook and shifted, chalk and erasers would not stay on the chalk-tray. Miss Plumley had a hard time keeping the attention of the children on their books, but the interruptions gave drama and zest to what had been dull and humdrum school life before.

That afternoon Orvie took his books home, intending to do his homework and get caught up, but there were interruptions there too. The men had just finished laying pipes to the Robinson house for gas.

"Golly!" he exclaimed, as the man lighted the gas burners in the new kitchen stove for the first time. "You can cook on it without wood?"

"I won't know how to act," said Mama, dabbing her eyes with her apron.

"Will it *explode*?" cried Addie, looking scared.

"Course not," said Della. "You just turn the handles off and on."

"It will take me a long time to get used to it," said Mama.

"Now I won't have nothing to do," said Orvie, smiling. He thought of the cords and cords of wood he had chopped for the old cook-stove that now sat out in the yard under the cottonwood tree. He thought of the hours of time he had spent chopping it.

"And to think there was plenty of gas down under our farm the whole time, and I never knew it!"

There was a bright gas light in every room now, with an up-turned glass shade. Each light burned from what was called a jet. Papa lighted them all and the family walked from room to room to look at the glow. The lights shone with golden brilliance even in the daytime.

"No more kerosene lamps to clean and fill, Della," laughed Grandpa.

"I'm not sorry," cried Della. "I'll hide the old lamps away in the attic where we'll never see them again."

"Now, ain't you glad we drilled for oil, Jennie?" asked Grandpa.

"Yes Pa," said Mama, dabbing her eyes again.

"We'll put in a telephone next," said Grandpa.

"A telephone! Oh my!" said Mama.

Orvie called to Della: "Know who the new tool-dresser is at

No. 2?"

"Who? Slim?" asked Della, blushing.

"Yes," said Orvie. "He told me to tell you. I'll go out now and tell him I told you."

Orvie jumped on his bicycle and rode out to No. 2 Robinson. But Slim was busy and could not see him. The boilerman whose job it was to tend the steam boilers was sick and had not come, so Slim was taking his place. The engine housing had not yet been built, so Orvie could see from a distance that Slim was occupied.

Nobody knew how it happened, but some one said afterwards that the water level had been allowed to get too low before re-filling the hot boiler, and this produced a flash of steam beyond the capacity of the safety valve. Suddenly the steam boiler exploded with a mighty roar, and Slim was thrown two hundred yards off into the slush-pond.

Orvie screamed. *"Slim!"* he yelled, pointing. *"Slim, oh Slim!"*

The men yelled and ran too, but Orvie was the first one there. He was sure they would pick Slim up dead or broken in pieces. He watched while the men helped Slim up, covered with mud and water from head to toe. Slim could walk, so he wasn't killed.

"Hey, kid, get to a telephone quick!" ordered Heavy, the driller. "You got one at your house?"

"No," said Orvie, "but we're gonna get one."

Slim was walking along, supported by two of the men.

"Where's the nearest telephone?" yelled the driller angrily.

"Oh, er . . ." Orvie tried to think. "The Murrays . . . no, they ain't got one . . . Old Pickering, yes the Pickerings had one put in . . . across the road and down a piece . . ."

"Get on your bike, go and telephone quick!" ordered Heavy.

"Who should I call up?" Orvie, already on his bicycle, yelled back over his shoulder.

"The ambulance, you nitwit, and do it quick before Slim dies!" came the answer.

Before Slim dies . . . before Slim dies . . . The words ringing in his head made Orvie's legs pump faster and harder than they had ever pumped before. "Oh, I never thought anything like this would happen to Slim . . . he could still walk . . ."

Orvie was half way to the Pickerings when he remembered that they had moved away, and the place was now a dance hall. Should he go in a wicked place like that? He knew Mama wouldn't want him to, but there must be a telephone there, and it was the nearest and the quickest.

Before Slim dies . . . before Slim dies . . . he pedaled faster.

He didn't have time to look at the verandah that had been all glassed in around the front, nor to notice the shiny floor varnished for dancing. All he saw was a tall thin man, with loose shaggy hair.

"Telephone!" he cried out. *"Telephone!"*

It was lucky for Orvie that he had memorized the signs stuck on telephone poles on the way into town. Now, one of them came back to him just when he needed it: *Ambulance phone 473.* He got an answer right away, and a man said they would come at once to No. 2 Robinson.

Orvie hung the receiver up and sank limply down into a chair

"Somebody hurt?" The long thin man stood beside him.

"Slim! Slim Rogers," said Orvie. "There was an explosion and he got blowed into the slush-pond. He musta got burned or something. He could still walk, but he never said one word . . ."

"Too bad," said the long thin man. He sat down at the piano and began to play softly.

Orvie stared at him. "Is it you makes all that loud music?"

"Part of it," said the man. "We have other instruments too." He stopped playing and looked at his own hands. "The tips of my fingers are all calloused," he said. "That comes of having to play all night long."

"You play all night long?" asked Orvie.

"Yes," said the man. "Can you hear it over at your house?"

"Yes," said Orvie. He knew the man wanted him to say something nice, so he added. "It sounds beautiful—I like it."

The man's sad face broke into a smile. "I'm glad," he said.

"Some folks say we ought to try to get rid of your dance hall," Orvie went on, "because you have drinking, gambling and dancing going on over here. But we never hear any loud noise nor yelling—only music, so Grandpa says we can't complain. Your music's pretty—it can't harm us none. I wish Della could hear it —she wants a piano, so she can take music lessons."

The man smiled again. He turned to the piano and began to play as Orvie ran off to his bicycle.

When he got back to the oil well, the ambulance was there, and Slim was lying on a stretcher. He smiled at Orvie but did not speak.

"Is he hurt bad?" demanded Orvie.

But Heavy and the other men did not answer. They loaded the stretcher into the ambulance. Its rear door closed with a bang, and its siren began to screech as it rolled out into the road. Orvie had seen ambulances go screeching by many times before. It was a common enough sight in the oil field, and had not meant anything. Now it was different.

"Is he hurt bad?" Orvie asked again.

"Don't know," said the driller. His voice, usually so cross, was kinder now. "Hope not. You go tell your sister what happened."

"Della?"

"Yes," said Heavy. "Slim will want her to come to the hospital to see him, you bet."

"Are they takin' him to the hospital?" asked Orvie.

"Sure," said the driller. "They'll fix him up in no time."

"Drilling oil wells is dangerous work," said Orvie.

"Sure is," said the driller.

Della cried and cried when she heard the news. She cried again when she came back from her first visit to the Tonkawa hospital. Slim was badly burned on his back and legs, and had to have considerable skin grafted on. He was to be in the hospital for two months or longer.

"Two months," said Orvie. "I'll sure miss him."

CHAPTER IX

Basket Picnic

"I HEAR you're havin' a basket picnic, so I come early."

Orvie held the school door open. "We're not ready yet," he said.

"Oh, Mrs. Soaper, I'm glad to see you," called Miss Plumley. "Come right in."

Mrs. Soaper marched in, followed by little Annie, age four, and Georgie, three. She carried a large basket in her hand.

"Oh Ma," cried Charley from his seat. "You're too early."

"We got a ride with that machine-shop man," said Mrs. Soaper. "No other way to get here. Good thing I came early, I can help you get ready. Here you, Freckles, sweep this mud out." She thrust the school broom into the boy's hand. "And you girls, bring some water and we'll scrub the floor."

"Pump's broke, Ma," said Charley. "Can't get no water."

"Dust up this mess then, girls."

Soon everybody was working under Mrs. Soaper's direction.

"Ralph, you and Orvie take the two doors off their hinges," said Miss Plumley. "Lay them over the desks to make a long table. Bonnie Jean and Ruth, get out your table cloths, and Lorita, bring that bunch of flowers for a center piece."

It was the last day of school. Now that the end had come, Orvie wished school would last longer. He enjoyed watching the oil drilling from the window beside his desk. But most of the parents thought it too dangerous for the children to have an oil well so close to the building, and other locations for more wells were being staked off in the schoolyard.

Charley Soaper stood by the open door to welcome the parents as they came, and Ruth Wilkins directed them to place cakes and pies at one end of the table, and main dishes at the other. Each mother brought plates enough for her own children. Orvie's mother was too busy to come, but had sent a large basket. Mrs. Soaper opened her basket and took out a large mixing bowl filled with coleslaw.

"Cabbage is cheap and fillin'," she said.

"I'm hungry!" begged Annie Soaper. "But I don't want slaw."

"I want a piece of pie," cried Georgie Soaper.

They stared at the array of food as if they had never had anything to eat in their lives.

At eleven-thirty Miss Plumley called everybody in and began the program. Like the regular school work, it was interrupted by loud bursts of steam from the engine by the oil well. But everybody was patient, and the children did their best.

Rosy Woods sang a song and the First Grade spoke a piece in unison. The older children produced a funny burlesque play called "The King of the Cannibal Isles" to loud applause. The entire school sang various selections while Miss Plumley played the piano. The singing of *America* ended the program.

Old Biddy Bascom appeared on her crutches just as lunch was ready.

"Hello, Orvie, my boy!" she cried. "And Freckles—another of my boys."

They dodged to escape her embarrassing pats. Everybody stared at the boarding-house keeper, as she was a newcomer in town. She wore her queer costume with long pantaloons beneath, green stockings and galoshes. Gray wisps of her hair stuck out from under her flopping sunbonnet.

"Where's your basket, Miz Bascom?" asked Mrs. Soaper.

"Didn't bring none," said Biddy. "Too far to tote it."

"But folks round here never come to a basket picnic without a basket!" scolded Mrs. Soaper. "Who do you think you are?"

Miss Plumley spoke up hurriedly. "Oh that's all right, Mrs. Soaper, we have twice as much food as we can eat. And you, Mrs. Bascom, you're very welcome, so don't give it another thought."

The two women glared at each other.

"Did you walk clear over from town, Mrs. Bascom?" asked Mrs. Barnes, trying to be friendly.

"No, I hitch-hiked!" Biddy cackled loudly. "Got three lifts and hopped the rest of the way."

Everybody found seats and the dishes were passed around. Soon young and old were busily eating. Charley Soaper dropped a hard-boiled egg on the floor and ducked under the table to get it. He came up with a howl on the other side.

"Poor Charley, how'd you get that big old knot on your head?" asked his mother.

"Orvie kicked me," yelled Charley.

"Never touched you," said Orvie.

"Then Freckles done it," yelled Charley.

"No I never," answered Freckles.

"You ought to know how to fall on the floor without hittin' your head, by this time," said Mrs. Soaper.

"Didn't fall—they kicked me!" retorted Charley.

"Boys will be boys!" cried Biddy Bascom, glaring at Charley's mother.

Orvie took two sandwiches and went out the open door. There on the front steps below the porch Nellie Jo and Edna Belle Murray were sitting. They were dressed in new and expensive dresses that looked wrong somehow.

"What you sittin' out here all alone for?" demanded Orvie.

"We're not allowed to talk," said Edna Belle.

"What's the matter—cat got your tongue?" asked Orvie.

"No," replied Nellie Jo.

"Miss Plumley scold you?"

"No," said Edna Belle.

"Why then?"

"It's because we're so rich," said Nellie Jo. "Mama told us not to talk to other people. They might try to kidnap us."

"Kidnap—what's that?" asked Orvie.

"Don't *you* know?" said Edna Belle. "I didn't either, but I know now. They'll take us and hide us, and make our Papa give 'em a lot of money before they bring us back."

"I don't want to be kidnapped," said Nellie Jo, starting to cry.

Orvie looked at the two girls. "Your Papa's oil money is not makin' you very happy, is it?"

"No," whispered Edna Belle. "I wish we'd never got rich."

"I'd rather be poor like the Soapers," said Nellie Jo in a faint voice. "They're poor and dirty, but they have fun. We can't do anything."

Orvie remembered how he used to tease the two girls. Now he felt sorry for them, and wished he could do something to help them. "You had anything to eat?" he asked.

"No," said Edna Belle. "We left our basket in there on the table. Our Mama wouldn't come, and we were afraid to talk to anybody else."

"Here, take these." Orvie thrust his two sandwiches into their hands. "I'll go and get you some more stuff." He went in and returned with two plates heaped high with food.

The Murray girls ate well after all, and went home happier than they had been in a long time.

After the picnic dinner was eaten and the tables were cleared away, Miss Plumley and the boys arranged a cake-walk. Ralph Wilkins put numbers on the floor in a circle, and the girls numbered all the cakes. Ralph Wilkins held up one cake, while Bonnie Jean and Ruth went around selling five cent chances on it. Then Miss Plumley played the piano, while those who had bought chances walked around the circle. When the music suddenly stopped, the person standing on the same number as the cake, won it.

It was great fun and everybody clapped and laughed. Freckles Hart took in the nickels, and as each cake brought in nearly a dollar, and there were fifteen cakes, Miss Plumley had the sum of fifteen dollars in her pocket-book before the afternoon was over. She said it would be used for a new pump in the school-yard when school reopened in the fall. If the school was moved to a new location because of the oil wells, it would be used for a new pump there.

Then the last day of school came to an end, and everybody

went home.

Orvie walked back over the prairie. The wheat fields were getting yellower each day as the grain ripened. In a few weeks, it would be time for harvest. Papa and Bert had already cut the alfalfa, which had been damaged by too much rain.

Orvie went into the barn and came out on Star's back. He wanted to ride. He called Shep and soon they went flying off over the back pasture. Shep ran back and forth sniffing.

"What are you after, Shep?" called Orvie. "A jackrabbit?" Then he saw the coyotes. *"Shep! Shep! Come back here, Shep!"*

But it was no use. The dog was after the coyotes now and he soon disappeared with them in the blackjack oaks.

Orvie patted Star and rode on. He didn't want to go to Cottonwood creek where the campers lived. But Harry Big Bear had told him that there were no campers on the creek in the Indian Reservation, and frog-hunting was good.

He rode on up toward the high part of the pasture. Up on the rise was a prairie-dog town. He could hear the little dogs barking. Sometimes when he rode past, fifty dogs about the size of squirrels would be sitting up straight, each at the hole of his burrow, barking.

Star came up over the brow of the hill so swiftly she stepped into a burrow and fell. Over her head went Orvie, down into the dust.

"Golly!" he cried. "Didn't know we were so close."

He picked himself up and ran to see if Star was hurt. Her leg and foot seemed to be all right. Good thing she had not broken her leg. Orvie turned to look at the dog-town. There were hundreds of holes, covered with mounds of gravel and red clay, but there was not a prairie-dog to be seen.

"I know you're in there!" cried the boy. He ran and got a pig-weed stalk and began poking it into a burrow. "You got rattle-snakes, owls and weasels down in there too. You're all eatin' each other up. I'll get you out. You can't hide from me down there."

He could not get them out, so he threw the stick down. He stood for a minute on the hill and looked around.

The rushing wind made a sound that told of loneliness and far places. Where was it coming from and where was it going? He remembered his short ride in the airplane, when he had soared high above the earth. Now, standing on the wind-swept hill, with the wide open prairie on all sides, he felt the same ecstasy. He knew the wonder of the world where men and birds soared in the sky; where the bounty of the earth furnished food for man and beast alike and where even the depths yielded treas-ures for man's use—precious stones, coal—and now oil.

Suddenly the bigness of the world frightened him and made him feel very small. He felt lonesome and afraid and hungry. He jumped on his pony's back and urged her on. He turned once and looked back.

All the prairie-dogs were out again barking at him. It was so funny he had to laugh.

He urged Star on. She crossed the Blackwell road, followed a path along Cottonwood creek and entered the Indian Reserva-tion. The creek was overgrown and shadier here. It was cooler, and there were no people. He could see the roof of White Cloud's house through the trees. He tied Star to a tree in the shade. Large bull-frogs sat on lily pads in the creek, croaking.

"Harry! Harry!" Orvie called as loud as he could.

Soon he heard a scuffle in the brush and Lily Wild Berry appeared.

"Where's Harry? Go tell him I want to catch frogs," said Orvie.

"I go get him." Lily darted off again.

She brought Harry, and Harry brought fish-poles and lines with hooks on the end. Orvie waded in the water until he was about fifteen feet away from a big bull-frog, sitting on a lily pad. He jiggled the hook till he got it under the frog's chin, then jerked the pole. Lily brought a tow sack and held it open while Orvie took the frog off the hook.

Harry was more expert than Orvie at catching frogs. He talked and laughed, telling how he trapped skunks and possums in the wintertime. It seemed like old times once again. Orvie was happier than he had been since oil was struck in the neighborhood.

A large cottonwood tree had been blown down and now lay across the creek, reaching from one high bank to the other. The earth had been washed away from its roots by the rain, and the trunk made a natural bridge over the creek. Orvie looked up at it.

"Dare you to walk that log!" he called out to Harry. "I dare you, I double-dare you . . ."

"Huh!" said Harry. "That ain't nothing." He did not move.

"I dare *you*, Lily," Orvie went on. "Double-dare you."

Lily looked up and shrugged her shoulders. She had brought a sharp knife and was busily cleaning the frogs already caught.

"Harry . . ." Orvie began, then he stopped suddenly, for he heard voices. "Golly! People comin' to spoil our fun. Bet it's some of those awful campers."

[123]

He ran up the dirt bank and to his surprise, saw not campers but a little girl. It was Bonnie Jean Barnes and a man following behind her who must be her father, Bill Barnes the shooter.

They said they wanted to go frog-hunting too, so Harry and Orvie turned over their poles and lines. When Bonnie Jean caught a frog, she squealed and danced. Then she sat down to watch Lily take it off the hook.

"I always did like frogs' legs to eat," cried Bonnie Jean.

"You eat plenty," said Lily. "You take 'em all home."

"My Daddy will catch enough for us," said Bonnie Jean. "Daddy and I just love to go frog-hunting, but Mama won't cook 'em at home."

"*You* can cook them," said Orvie. "I know how, I'll show you."

Bonnie Jean opened her eyes up wide. "*You* know how—a boy?"

"Sure," boasted Orvie. "I know lots of things."

Bonnie Jean and her father stayed and stayed because they enjoyed it so much. Bill Barnes told the boys he had been "a shooter" for twenty years and he knew his business, but he liked a vacation from it now and then. He liked to go off swimming or fishing—or frog-hunting.

"Why do you 'shoot' wells, anyhow?" asked Orvie.

"Tell us," begged Harry.

"Well, boys, sometimes there is oil down in the well," said Bill Barnes, "but it's lodged tight in the oil rock and they can't get it out. We have to make an artificial earthquake down there to start the flow of oil. This is called 'shooting the well.' We fill the well with three or four hundred feet of water, and let the torpedoes down to the water and unhook them to flow in the rest of the way. Then we drop a go-devil down to explode it. This busts the oil rock up into pieces. Then the oil flows through the cracks into the well."

"Golly!" said Orvie. "So that's how they do it."

"That's how *I* do it," said Bill Barnes. "We have a fancy name for the dynamite we use—nitro-glycerin. It looks like common glycerin, and we put twenty-five to one hundred quarts of it into long narrow metal buckets called shells, which are lowered by a cable. It's ticklish stuff to handle. When you haul it, if you give it the least little bump, it will explode and go off. That means goodbye for you."

The boys' faces grew sober.

"Gee!" said Orvie, after a pause. "It must be wonderful to be a shooter."

"As long as you're careful," added the man. "We're always careful, ain't we, Bonnie Jean? The accident always happens to the other fellow, don't it?"

The little girl ran and threw her arms around her father, and Orvie could see a cloud of worry like a shadow on her face. He knew now that she lived always in the fear of danger—in the fear of death.

"I dare you to cross that log—I dare you!" Harry came beside him, yelling.

Orvie ran up the bank, jumped on the fallen tree and holding his arms out to balance himself, walked slowly over. Half-way across he began to shake—the water looked dark and scary so far below. He kept on.

"Double-dare you to come back again," yelled Harry Big Bear.

A dare always had to be met, so he walked slowly back over the log.

Bill Barnes and Bonnie Jean were getting ready to go. "Come, walk home with us," begged Bonnie Jean.

"I got my pony," said Orvie. "You can ride Star, Bonnie Jean, and I'll lead her."

"Come and have supper at our house," said Bill Barnes.

"We'll let you cook the frogs' legs," added Bonnie Jean.

Lily Wild Berry insisted they take the whole bagful. Barnes threw it over his shoulder and they started off.

"Yippy—yip—pee! Yippy—yip—pee!" came Harry's voice behind them.

Bonnie Jean climbed up on Star's back and the trio looked back. They saw the two Indian children, completely fearless, go flying across the log on a dead run.

"Yip—pee! Yip—pee!" called Orvie in reply.

When they reached the Osage Torpedo house, Mrs. Barnes repeated the invitation to supper. Bill Barnes spread the frogs' legs on the table, while Bonnie Jean and Orvie washed their hands and faces in the basin.

"Frog-hunting again," laughed Mrs. Barnes. "You know I can't cook them. They kick in the skillet and I can't stand it to watch them."

The others laughed.

Bonnie Jean tied an apron around Orvie's waist.

"Mama soaks 'em in salt water first," said Orvie, "to take out some of the kick. Then you put them in the skillet quick, cover it with a flat lid, and put a flatiron on top to keep them down. If they kick, you'll never see it. They can't kick hard enough to kick the lid off!"

Bonnie Jean and her father and mother laughed and laughed. Orvie stayed for supper and everybody enjoyed the frogs' legs except Mrs. Barnes, who ate scrambled eggs.

CHAPTER X

Whizzbang

"WHERE'D that jackrabbit go to?" asked Orvie. "Did we run over him?"

"Didn't hear a bump," said Bert. "He ran under the car, didn't he?"

Orvie and Bert were in the Ford, on their way to town. Orvie looked back. "Can't see him. We didn't run over him, and I can't see him in either of the ditches. Wonder where he disappeared to."

They laughed and thought nothing more of it just then.

It was a hot day in August, and the road which in April had been a sea of mud was now deep in dust. All the grass in the pastures was brown and dry, and the wheat stubble had been plowed under. The fields were sprinkled with oil derricks, and these were surrounded by oil-laden ponds and ditches. There had been no rain for a long time, and there was little evidence of green growth.

The Ford rattled into Whizzbang and Bert parked in front of Peg-Leg Moore's store.

When Orvie got out of the car the first thing he saw was Slim Rogers sitting in a rocking chair on the front porch of Biddy Bascom's boarding house across the street.

"Hi, Slim!" called Orvie. "Golly, Slim! You all well again?"

"I'm fine, Orvie," answered Slim. "Got back from the hospital yesterday. Got a new hide on my back and legs. Nothing wrong except . . ."

"What is it, Slim? Anything I can do for you?" Orvie hurried over.

"I'm just hungry, boy, for some good home cooking," confessed Slim. "Terrible stuff they fed me in that hospital. And here—Biddy is all right, but she don't go to much trouble—just throws food together, and it don't taste right."

"Mama's cooking's awful good, Slim," said Orvie. "So's Della's."

Slim laughed. "I bet Della makes good rabbit gravy!"

"She sure does," said Orvie.

Orvie took the bottles of milk and a basket of eggs into Biddy Bascom's kitchen. When he came out, Slim stopped him.

"Got me a pair of new driller boots," he said, "with steel cap safety toes." Orvie gazed at the boots in admiration. "For protection against falling objects, so I won't get my toes mashed. Say, Orvie, will you take a message to your sister?"

"Sure will," said Orvie.

"Tell her she's gonna have company for dinner tomorrow," said Slim. "Don't tell her who's comin', but she better have rabbit gravy."

"Sure—rabbit gravy, I'll tell her." Orvie laughed. "So long, Slim."

He crossed over the street.

"Got to do Mama's tradin'," he called to Bert. He bent over to put the egg basket on the back seat of the car, and there, sitting on the running board, he saw a strange sight.

"Here's that crazy jackrabbit, Bert!" yelled Orvie. "He had a ride into town with us. What d'you know about that? Looky! There he goes!"

The jackrabbit took a flying leap across the board sidewalk and disappeared in the open door of Peg-Leg Moore's store. The next minute Orvie followed, and Freckles Hart followed Orvie. Other people followed Freckles, and a rabbit hunt was on.

Peg-Leg's business had doubled, so the store had twice as many groceries, and there were twice as many customers as usual. Violent commotion ensued.

Women screamed as the long-legged rabbit dashed down the main aisle, circled, and hurdled a showcase of candy and baked goods. The next minute he knocked over a pyramid of tomato cans on the counter and leaped over a rack of hoes and shovels. Women and children dodged, shrieking, and Peg-Leg ducked under the counter.

Suddenly the jackrabbit halted, hunched over on the floor as if breathless and exhausted. Orvie approached cautiously, Freckles behind him. Orvie reached out, grabbed a bunch of hair but did not get the rabbit. *Crash, smash, bang!* Bunny made a leap through the glass in the front show window.

"Gone!" shouted Peg-Leg. "Gone!" echoed the customers. "He's off for the big wide prairie."

"Biggest jackrabbit I ever saw in my life!" cried Orvie, when he stopped laughing.

"He had to run sideways to keep from flyin'!" added Freckles.

"I'll sue that long-legged rabbit for damages!" laughed Peg-Leg, hurrying to get a broom to sweep up the broken glass.

Orvie took out of his pocket a piece of paper with a long list of groceries written on it. "Mama wants these," he said to the storekeeper.

Peg-Leg read the list over. "Looks like she's feedin' an army."

"Pretty near," said Orvie. "Two sittings every meal and nothing much left over for us kids. I got eggs and chickens in the Ford to trade." He went out to bring them in.

When he reached the board sidewalk, he stopped dead in his tracks. There sat Bert in the front seat of the Ford, roaring with laughter, holding up a jackrabbit by its hind legs.

"Golly!" exclaimed Orvie. "Is that *him?*"

"Killed hisself buttin' his head through the window!" laughed Bert. "Landed smack in my lap!"

"Haw, haw, haw!" Slim Rogers, who had been watching the excitement from his reserved seat on the front porch across the street, called out: "Take him home with you, Orvie, and remember I ordered gravy!"

"Sure thing, Slim!" shouted Orvie.

He took the eggs and chickens back in the store where Peg-Leg was piling up Mama's groceries.

"Bunny never made the wide open spaces that time," laughed the storekeeper.

"No, he made Mama's frying pan!" laughed Orvie.

"See my new wooden leg?" asked the storekeeper. "Just come yesterday from the factory."

"Gee, it sure looks fine," said Orvie, peering over the counter. "All that varnish and everything. Bet it cost a lot. How does it make you feel?"

"Frisky as that jackrabbit!" laughed Peg-Leg. "Makes me want to take to the prairie too, but I think I'll go through the door instead of the window."

"So will I," said Orvie, carrying the groceries out to the Ford. Freckles helped by bringing a twenty-five pound bag of flour.

"I'll get your milk now, Freckles," said Orvie, "and take it to the Café. You just wait a minute."

The Bucking Horse was right next door. Freckles waited obligingly.

"Don't stay all day," growled Bert.

Freckles opened the restaurant door and the two boys found it cool and quiet inside. A man sat at the counter, while several others lounged at tables. Some sat with their heads on their folded arms, where they had been sleeping all night.

"What? No shootin' today?" asked Orvie.

"Well, there's the Chief," said Freckles. "He's the driller that Hooky Blair and Two-Gun Jimmy got it in for. They ordered him out of town and he's still here. Hang around a while—he might start something."

"He better do it quick," said Orvie. "I gotta get back before Bert skins me alive."

They stared, but the man was sitting quietly, eating his dinner. Orvie took the milk to the kitchen and came back.

"Aw, stay around a while. Something's always happening here, honest," promised Freckles.

"I'll stay till Bert comes after me," said Orvie.

The place was so quiet and still, it seemed unlikely anything could happen. But just then, two men entered the restaurant. One wore high-heeled cowboy boots and the other had a hook for a hand. The Chief looked up and saw them. He rose slowly from his stool, took money from his pocket and paid the cashier for his meal. The cashier turned white and looked scared. An atmosphere of tension came over the room. The men at the tables looked up, but no one moved.

As the Chief approached the two men, they backed quickly out the door. Like a flash, he followed.

"That was Hooky and Two-Gun!" cried Freckles. "Let's see what the Chief's up to." The boys made a bee-line for the door.

A sudden shot rang out. One of the two men fell on the board-walk outside, the other ran away. The Chief ran after the second man and fired several times. The two men kept on running and others joined in the chase.

In front of the Bucking Horse Café, a crowd quickly gathered around the fallen man.

"What did I tell you?" asked Freckles proudly.

"Did somebody kill somebody?" asked Orvie.

Freckles ducked into the circle of people and came back.

"It's Hooky Blair," he announced. "The Chief shot him."

"Is he dead?" asked Orvie.

"Looks dead enough to me," said Freckles. "Now you've seen a man get killed."

"I ain't even had a look at him yet," said Orvie.

[133]

"Better hurry, they're gonna load him in that wagon," said Freckles.

Somebody grabbed Orvie by the arm. He looked up and saw that it was Bert.

"Orvie, you come right back to the car," ordered Bert. "We got to get out of here quick."

"Just a minute, Bert," said Orvie. "I want to see something."

"Mama said you're not to be hangin' around these here tough places," scolded Bert. "I saw them fellers shootin' and I'm goin' home right away."

Orvie felt he could not go just yet. He had to satisfy his curiosity. He jerked loose from Bert, came up to the edge of the crowd and forced his way in. The crowd parted and he could see plainly. He saw Hooky Blair lying dead on the ground. He saw his outstretched arm with the hook on it. He saw the man's white face and his open mouth. He saw spots of blood on his neck and shirt. It was enough. He didn't want to see anything more.

Orvie turned and edged back through the crowd. Men were picking the body up and putting it into a two-horse wagon. Freckles had gone. Orvie stumbled back toward the car. He knew Bert would be furious with waiting.

He stopped in the gutter behind the Ford and vomited. He was sick half the way home.

Bert stared at Orvie's white face. "I hope you're satisfied," he said.

Orvie was. Now he knew why Mama had wanted him to stay away. Mama was right. He would stay as far away as he could after this. He never wanted to see a shooting again.

*   *   *

There were several calls to make on the way home. The Murray house was closed up, and had all the blinds pulled down. Orvie thought they must have gone away. He knocked at the back door to see if they wanted any milk.

He waited and waited. He knocked more loudly.

Suddenly a door at the side of the house opened and two large police dogs dashed out. They barked furiously and snapped at Orvie's heels as he ran, almost dropping his bottles. Looking back, he saw the heads of the two little girls peeping out from under a window shade.

Orvie knew now. They hadn't gone away at all. They were hiding in there with all their fears. The dogs were to protect the little girls. They weren't allowed out of the house any more. Orvie thought of the fun he and Addie were always having together. "I'd rather be us," he thought, "than two little fat girls with lots of money." He set the bottles of milk down at the edge of the lawn.

"Them cross old dogs like to tore me up," he said to Bert, as he jumped back in the car.

Bert made some stops along the row of little houses. When they came to the house in the alfalfa field, where Hazel and Jack Daley lived, Orvie saw bedding stretched out on a clothesline.

He stared hard at it. There was the blue checked quilt he used to have on his own bed. Next to it was the pink-flowered quilt from Della's bed. He remembered the day when Mama had missed them off her own clothesline and said she was living in "a nest of thieves." It was the same day Orvie and Charley had sold the whisky bottles to Nicky Grimes, the bootlegger. He could never forget that.

Orvie knew Mama would be glad to get the bedding back again. He marched boldly into Hazel Daley's house and was surprised to see how small it was. It held an iron bed, a table, two chairs, a heating stove and a small gas plate, a wash stand and a cupboard. Hazel Daley was sitting on the edge of the bed, dressed in a bright red kimono, combing out her light yellow hair. Orvie thought she looked pretty, even though he was mad at her.

"Where did you get those quilts on the line, Mrs. Daley?" he demanded.

"Where did I get 'em?" answered Hazel. "Why, I made 'em myself!" She stared at the boy from head to toe. "What business is it of yours, I'd like to know?"

"You? You made 'em?" sniffed Orvie. "Why, you can't even sew a stitch. I heard you tell Mrs. Soaper you never darn Jack's stockings. When they get holes in 'em, you just throw 'em away."

Orvie thumped the bottle of milk down in the middle of the floor and walked out.

"Well, my pretty young man, and who are you? *Judge* Robinson, I suppose!" came the woman's sarcastic voice behind him.

Orvie jumped from the doorstep, grabbed the quilts from the line and ran for the car. Hazel Daley took time to pick up a broom, and then, with her long hair flying, chased swiftly after him.

"You bring back them quilts, bring 'em back I say! You'll be sorry, Orvie Robinson. Orvie Robinson, you'll be sorry!" she shouted.

Luckily Bert had kept the engine going. Orvie threw the bedding in the back and jumped in front. "Hurry, Bert, hurry, she's after me!" A volley of stones, thrown by the angry woman, showered over the Ford.

"What's the matter with Hazel Daley?" asked Bert. "She crazy?"

"No, just mad," said Orvie. "She *stole* those quilts and I'm takin' 'em back. They're Mama's and she can't have 'em."

Bert grunted.

"What do you s'pose she meant when she said I'd be sorry?" Orvie asked.

"Dunno," said Bert.

When the boys reached home, Orvie ran into the house with the quilts. Mama was on her hands and knees, scrubbing the kitchen floor.

"Are these yours, Mama?" asked Orvie.

Mama got up and sat on a chair. "Yes," she said. "Where did you find 'em?"

After Orvie told his story, Mama said, "That Hazel Daley. She's a dishonest woman—takin' quilts off my clothesline in broad daylight. Seems like you boys are late getting home. Anything happen in town?"

"No . . . er, well, no . . ." Orvie hesitated. "Nothin' much."

He didn't like to tell about the Murray girls shut up in their house or mention the shooting. He knew Mama wouldn't like that.

"You sure?" Mama looked at him hard.

"Oh, I almost forgot," said Orvie. "We chased a jackrabbit through Peg-Leg's store . . . and I saw Slim!"

"Slim!" Della came out of the dining room.

"You're going to have company for dinner tomorrow, Della," Orvie went on, "and you're to be sure and have rabbit gravy."

Della flushed to the roots of her hair.

"We brought you the rabbit—it went *whizz-bang* right through Peg-Leg's front show window and Bert caught it!"

"Can Slim come, Mama?" asked Della.

"He's starved for home cooking," added Orvie.

"Bless his heart," said Mama. "Of course he can come. We'll

[138]

cook him up a good meal."

When Slim came the next day, he said the gravy was the best he ever ate. They all had a happy time together, and it was good to have Slim back. He told them that he would soon be going to work on No. 5 Murray.

"What? You goin' right back on the job?" said Papa. "After that accident of yours, I'd think you'd want to be a farmer or do something safe, and give up this oil business."

"It's such greasy, dirty work, Slim," said Della. "Couldn't you find something cleaner?"

Slim laughed. "Nope—oil's in my blood, I guess. I'd never be happy at anything else. When you know the best and worst of anything, it's got you for keeps."

Orvie was never to forget Slim's words.

The very next morning Orvie found out what Hazel Daley meant by her final retort. About mid-day, Jim Duncan drove into the yard in his huckster wagon. Jim sold cakes, rolls, cookies and pies, making stops at all the oil field houses. He had a good trade with people who had no transportation to the stores in the towns.

"Mrs. Robinson," he called out, "where's them folks gone to that used to live in that shack in the alfalfa field? Daley, their name was. Where are they?"

Mama came to the door. "They're not there?"

"Hazel hasn't been up here for water this morning," said Orvie. "I been watchin' out for her."

"They're not there," said Jim Duncan, "not hide nor hair of 'em. Their house is empty. I walked in when I saw the front door open. They left in the middle of the night, the neighbor said. I thought you might know where they've gone to."

"Gone?" cried Mama. "They haven't paid their rent. She told me she'd pay up next week and I believed her. I'll go right down there."

"The neighbors say they owe everybody—restaurant, dry goods, millinery and all the other stores," said Duncan. "They pay a little down and forget to pay the rest. They owe me for baked goods for three weeks." Jim got back in his wagon and took up the lines.

"Can't you sue 'em?" called Orvie.

"Can't sue 'em when you can't find 'em," said Duncan angrily. He whipped up his horse and drove off.

Orvie went to the house in the alfalfa field with Mama. The furniture that was left was broken to pieces.

"Here's something, Mama." Orvie ducked under the ramshackle bed and pulled out six large cardboard boxes, one by one. Mama opened them and found six fancy hats.

"A lot of good they'll do me," said Mama. "I'd like to put 'em on a bonfire. But since they're not paid for and haven't been worn much, I'll take them back to the Sunflower Dept. store."

"So that's why she said I'd be sorry," remarked Orvie. "She ran off without paying the rent. Hazel Daley—such a pretty woman too."

He remembered what Grandpa had said—it takes all kinds of people to make up a world.

CHAPTER XI

A Big Time

"You hold her tail now, Addie, while I milk," said Orvie.
"How can I hold it when I'm shooin' flies off?" said Addie,
waving a pigweed stalk back and forth.

The cow's tail jerked violently and slapped Orvie in the face.
He fell backward off his stool. "Now looky there . . ." He put
his hand up to his reddened cheek. "Golly! It burns like fire. I
know what I'll do—I'll tie her up."

He brought a rope and tied the cow's tail to her hind leg. Addie
kept on shooing flies and Orvie resumed his milking.

"Are we poor?" asked Addie suddenly. "Is that why Papa won't
never give us more'n a nickel to spend?"

The question surprised Orvie. "I don't know," he said, after a
pause. "I'll ask Grandpa."

They stopped under the cottonwood tree and put the question to the old man. Grandpa stared at the two children and scratched his head.

"Poor? Who said we are poor?" he answered. "Now that reminds me of something, and today is as good a time as any." He took a piece of paper from his pocket and went into the kitchen, followed by the children. He waved the paper in the air.

"Jennie, how do you like your new gas stove?" he asked.

Mama mopped her brow. "I guess I'll like it, once I get used to it," she said. "It cooks so fast I burn everything up, and I keep thinking it might explode."

"You better get used to it," said Grandpa, " 'cause it's yours. I paid up all the payments on it."

"Oh Pa," said Mama. "You're so good to us."

Grandpa called Papa and Bert in from the yard. They hated to leave the big shiny new automobile that stood there, but they came.

"I want you to go to town today and have a big time," said Grandpa. "I want you to buy *everything you want!* See this little piece of paper? I'll put my name to it, and we'll go to the bank first and I'll fill your pocket-books full of cash, and you're to spend it—every cent. Don't come home until it's all gone."

The family stood still, open-mouthed with surprise. Addie jumped up and down, clapped her hands and said, "Goody! Goody!"

"There's plenty for everybody," said Grandpa. "Let's go buy the town out."

"Pa, are you serious?" asked Papa.

"Oh, but Pa . . ." Mama began. "You bought Al the new car and me the new stove . . . You save the rest for your old age."

[142]

"Nonsense," said Grandpa. "I'm a spring chicken. Don't I live in a hen-house? I want you folks to spend to your heart's content just this once."

Mama hurried to get ready. She went to the yard to bring in the washing. She had washed the night before and hung the clothes out before daylight to get them dry before the dust got so bad.

Della had to finish sweeping. "Seems like we're eatin' and breathin' dust," she said. "It keeps a body busy just sweeping."

"Everything's covered with dust—every leaf and branch and blade of grass," said Mama, coming in with her arms full of clothes. "We must shut all the doors and windows tight before we go."

"The Murrays keep their house shut up tight," said Orvie. "Looks just like everybody's gone away."

"That old oil company," growled Bert, shaving by the kitchen mirror, "cuttin' all them 'company roads' through our farm. You can hardly see them big wagons and trucks for the dust they make. You get dust whichever way the wind blows."

"And we have to sweep it out by the bucketful," added Della.

The family all dressed up in their Sunday clothes, and soon they were ready to start. Mama and Della left a cold lunch on the table for the boarders to eat, and put the key to the back door under the mat.

"We'll eat at a Café," suggested Grandpa. "We'll be stylish and dine out."

They piled into the new car. It was a deep maroon seven-passenger Packard sedan and had comfortable cushioned seats and a flaring open top.

"We'll get covered with dust, if we don't put the side-curtains on," said Della.

"If we put them on and close it up, we'll smother with the heat," said Bert.

"I like to feel the wind blow through," added Orvie.

"Maybe I should have took that closed model," said Papa. "But it looked so new-fangled, with glass windows all around."

"This new car is just right," said Mama. "Trust these kids to start complainin'."

"Stop your talkin'," ordered Grandpa, "so your Pa can think what he's doin'. Do you want us to land in the ditch?"

Papa drove slowly and intently in the ensuing silence. It was not easy to drive the new Packard after the old Ford, but he had been taking lessons and managed pretty well. The new car rolled along very smoothly, leaving a billowing cloud of dust behind it. It went straight through Whizzbang and Bliss and came to Ponca City.

"If we're goin' on a buyin' spree," said Grandpa, with a twinkle in his eye, "we may as well go to a city where there's a few things to *buy*. Nothin' worse than to *want* things and not be able to find what you want."

They parked in front of the largest bank in Ponca City, and they walked in through the big bronze doors. A smiling man with a bald head met Grandpa and ushered him inside an iron gate. Grandpa signed the check, and the man brought the money out and spread it over a table.

Grandpa picked up handfuls without counting and passed them out. Mama, Della and Addie all had pocket-books, which they stuffed full. Orvie, Bert and Papa filled their pockets. Part of the money was in silver—big silver dollars that clinked together, and part of it in bills. There was a lot of loose change for everybody too.

Grandpa waved his arm and shouted: "Go on out on your spending spree!" The people in the bank turned and looked.

Orvie remembered the nickels that Papa used to hand out so sparingly. It was hard for Papa to part with a nickel. Maybe that was because he had so few of them. He always made Orvie feel that a nickel was something very special, something he'd worked very hard to earn, something not to be thrown away or wasted or spent lightly. It was to be treasured, and whatever was bought with it, was to be treasured too. Orvie often ended up by not spending it at all. He couldn't find anything that was worthy of the wonderful nickel he carried in his pants pocket.

Now he began to wonder. Had they really been as poor as that? Were there so few nickels that Papa could spare one so rarely? When he had asked Grandpa if they were poor, Grandpa had not answered the question.

Orvie thought of the campers who lived on Cottonwood creek. He knew how little they had to eat and to wear, and how shabbily they lived. He thought of the oil workers' families in the little box-car houses. Some of them made high wages while the work lasted, but spent it quickly and were soon poor again. They had all their furniture in one room, and often had no more than enough to eat and wear.

Orvie saw his own family in perspective for the first time.

The Robinsons owned a farm and a seven-room house. They had all they could eat—their own hogs and beef to butcher, their own vegetables and fruit, and all the milk and cream and butter they could use. Orvie had never seen a member of his family dress in rags—except Grandpa, who wore ragged overalls to be comfortable, but had others that were not ragged or torn.

Were the Robinsons poor, or did they only think they were, because they worked hard for all the very real comforts they enjoyed? That was it. Papa *thought* they were poor. He and Mama had started out with very little, and they kept on thinking they were poor long after they had plenty. That was why it was such a struggle for Papa to give Orvie a nickel to spend. That was why Orvie had such a hard time spending it.

But now all that was over. Grandpa was going to cure the Robinsons of feeling poor all the time. Grandpa was going to make them spend. They could never act poor and think poor again, because from now on they were rich.

It gave Orvie a strange feeling of exhilaration as he walked

down the main street of Ponca City. The family had decided to separate and do their spending independently. All but Addie, who was to stay with Mama.

Orvie put his hands into his pockets and jingled the silver dollars against each other. He began to whistle. He felt happier than he had ever felt in his life before. His Sunday shirt chafed his neck, but he did not notice or care. He stopped at every show window and looked at everything in it. It was a grand feeling to think he could buy anything he saw.

The stores and streets were crowded with people. He saw Indian squaws wearing bright-colored shawls, and Indian men with braided hair. The Indians had money too—oil had been discovered on their lands. They rode in big cars, and their children had money in their pockets too.

Orvie walked up one side of the street and came back down the other. He felt hungry, so he stopped at a Café and bought a hot-dog, a ham and cheese sandwich, and a piece of cherry pie. He walked on, studying the windows. He picked out a mouth organ, a new saddle for Star and a pair of cowboy boots. He also chose new overalls, a fancy belt, some bandana handkerchiefs and a Stetson hat. That was all he wanted for himself. He decided to come back later to buy them.

He was hungry again, so he went in a drug store and bought a milkshake, a banana split and a raspberry soda. When he came out, he decided to think about presents for the rest of the family. He saw a box of silver knives and forks--that would do for Mama. A hat with pink roses—that would be for Della. Six cute little silk dresses—just the right size for Addie. He thought of the tractor that Bert wanted, but compromised on a pocket knife with six different blades.

All at once he saw Mama. She looked flushed and worried. Addie had three sacks of candy in each hand and was chewing noisily.

"How will we get everything home?" Orvie asked.

"Tell them to deliver it," said Mama.

"What did you buy, Mama?" Orvie asked.

"So many things I can't remember," said Mama. "Have you seen Della?"

"No Mama . . ." said Orvie.

A young lady came up. "Do I have the pleasure of addressing Mrs. Al Robinson?" she asked, making a deep bow.

"Why, Della! Why . . . Della!" cried Mama and Orvie together. "I thought for a minute you were Hazel Daley. What are you doing all decked out in clothes like that?"

"I bought them, Mama." Della swished around to show her new gown of Belgian blue crêpe de Chine, with long flowing sleeves, long, slinky skirt down to her ankles, and a squashy-looking hat with drooping feathers.

"Oh Della, what awful clothes!" gasped Mama. "They don't look right for a girl like you. Why didn't you get some new middy blouses?"

"I'm not a girl any longer," said Della. "I'm a rich young lady."

Mama stared at her, unbelieving.

"I bought a beautiful fur coat . . ." continued Della.

"Of genuine rabbit-skin?" laughed Orvie. "To keep you warm on the hottest day in summer?"

"You little pest!" scolded Della. "Don't you think I can keep it until winter comes? I bought a player-piano, too—fifteen dollars down and only thirteen dollars a month after that."

"Good land! A player-piano! What on earth?" asked Mama.

Grandpa came bustling up, fresh as a daisy. "Got everything you want, everybody? All ready to go eat? It's nearly three o'clock. But before we go home, I want to show you something on the way out of town."

They ate in style in a Café, but Orvie wasn't hungry. Dishes rattled and men talked in loud voices. Orvie let his plateful of food sit in front of him and get cold. As they left the restaurant, Orvie decided not to buy the things he had picked out, after all. It was too much trouble.

Following Grandpa's directions, Papa drove to a side street on the edge of town, and pulled up in front of a large red brick house.

"Who lives here?" asked Mama, peering out.

"There's nobody home today, but they said we could go in and look around," said Grandpa.

They got out of the car and went in the house, which Grandpa opened with a key. They walked over velvet carpets and peered through thick lace curtains. The house had running water and two bathrooms. It was completely furnished, but looked cold, empty and cheerless.

"It's very nice," said Mama, and they got in the car again. Papa drove faster now. He was getting used to the car. They went home by way of Tonkawa just for the ride.

When they came by the Prairie View Church, they saw a crowd of people in the churchyard. Two oil wells in the field behind were hammering away noisily.

"Looks like a funeral," said Mama. "Wonder whose it can be."

"We'll go in," said Papa. He parked the Packard inside the fence with the other cars. A high new fence of barbed wire encircled the churchyard, and two men with large clubs stood by the gate.

The funeral was over and flowers were being carried out to a freshly dug grave in the cemetery. The organist was still playing. Mama saw Liza Pickering and hurried over to her.

"Saddest funeral I ever been to," said Liza, wiping her eyes. "It's that little Soaper girl—Annie. Her mother'll never get over it."

"Mrs. Soaper's little girl is *dead?* The one they called Annie?" asked Mama. "And her funeral's over?"

It was true. The people were streaming back from the cemetery into the church yard.

"How did it happen?" asked Mama.

"Her two little children was playin' out in the yard," said Liza Pickering. "There was a leak in the gas pipe that went to their house, and they was spittin' at the leak to make bubbles. Pretty soon little Georgie run to the house and told his Mama that Annie had gone to sleep. They'd been leanin' over the leak and she breathed in the gas. It was a still day, no wind at all—day before yesterday. They took her to the Tonkawa hospital, but she was dead. That poor mother—she was wringin' her hands and screamin' something awful."

"She was my neighbor," said Mama slowly, "and I never knew about it until it was all over."

"Oh, they're only poor oil workers, Jennie," said Liza. "They spend their lives following the oil fields—he's just a roustabout. Here today and gone tomorrow."

"She was my neighbor," repeated Mama in a low voice, "and I never went to her when she needed me. What if she *was* poor? She loved her little one and lost her, and I was out *spending* . . ."

Liza said, "Let's go hear what them men are sayin' about drillin' in the cemetery. Did you see them guards with clubs?"

"What are they there for?" asked Mama.

"To keep the oil men out," said Liza.

The women went back of the church where the men were shouting in loud voices. Orvie followed his mother.

"I gave this land to the church," said Sandy Watkins. "My father took this quarter-section in the Cherokee Strip opening, and he and my mother are buried here. As long as the land is used for church and cemetery, it belongs to the congregation."

"But Sandy," said Walt Pickering. "With all the money we get from the oil company, we can buy land somewheres else and build a church ten times as big."

"But we live here, and we want our church here," spoke up a woman.

"Now friends, we'll locate one well ten feet this side of the cemetery and another one in that bare spot where nobody's buried."

"We've got our lease and we're going to drill. You can't keep us out!" shouted an important-looking man.

"Listen to those oil men!" said Mama to Liza.

"No, no, the women won't allow it," spoke up Sandy Watkins. "They say you're too close to the back fence as it is."

"You've got that whole Watkins lease . . ." began John Murray.

"But the churchyard and cemetery are a part of the Watkins lease," protested the oil man. "We've got a right to . . ."

"Your derricks are throwing shadows on the tombstones as it is—they're so close," John Murray went on quietly. "We ask you not to come any closer than you are now."

"Our guards will keep you out by force!" Grandpa Robinson

shook his fists in the oil men's faces.

The clamor of the oil wells kept on and on.

"Golly, let's go, Mama," said Orvie, "before they start fightin'."

The family waited in the Packard for Grandpa to come, and then drove home. Orvie went straight into Grandpa's little house under the cottonwood tree. He stood by the bed and turned his pants pockets inside out. He dumped the silver dollars, bills and change onto the bed.

"Hey, what you doin'?" asked Grandpa. "Didn't you do what I told you to do—spend it and get all the things you been wantin'?"

"I picked out lots of things, Grandpa," said Orvie, "and then . . . I didn't want 'em after all."

Grandpa patted him on the shoulder.

"Don't surprise me none!" he said.

CHAPTER XII

Summer Tragedy

"HELLO, everybody!" called a familiar voice. "Has Grandpa moved back into the house and decided to be civilized?"

Aunt Lottie and Uncle Mart stepped in, prepared to spend Sunday as usual. "Now that he's the richest man in the county . . . " Aunt Lottie stopped and looked around her. "Land sakes! What's all this? You folks startin' a furniture store?"

"No, Lottie," said Mama. "Grandpa gave us some money to spend. We've just been getting us a few little things we've been wanting."

The deliveries had rolled in all through the week. Hardly a day passed without the arrival of a purchase made by some member of the family. By Sunday, the Robinson house had a changed appearance.

For Della, fur coat, player-piano, fancy clothes and hats had arrived. For Mama, electric icebox, a new wash-machine, toaster, vacuum cleaner, dishes, silver, curtains and carpets. For Bert, an Edison phonograph, a radio and a drum. For Papa, two over-stuffed chairs and a sofa, twelve pairs of suspenders, and four new suits. For Addie, twelve dolls and all kinds of doll furnishings.

"It *is* a little crowded," said Mama, as she began to step over things to return to the kitchen. "I declare, the house just isn't big enough."

"Why don't you buy a new one?" asked Aunt Lottie. "Why don't you buy a house in town?"

"Oh Lottie, do you suppose we could?" asked Mama.

"Why not?" laughed Lottie. "The way you folks are throwin' money around . . ."

"It sure is nice to have millionaire relations!" laughed Uncle Mart.

"I just can't get used to spending," said Mama.

"You will in time," said Lottie. "Any time you have too much money, you know what you can do with it."

Mama took her pocket-book from behind the clock on the shelf. She brought out a handful of bills and gave them to her sister. "Here, I want you to get some nice things too."

Lottie stared at the money, astonished. "These are one hundred dollar bills, did you know that?"

"That's all right," said Mama. "I got plenty more."

"Well, I like the casual way you do it," laughed Lottie. "Remember the good old days when we had to save up for weeks to get things we really needed?"

"We had so little then," said Mama, "I couldn't even buy a

handkerchief without feeling I ought to do without it."

"I bet you wouldn't like to go back to that again," said Lottie.

"I wonder . . . how it would feel . . ." said Mama.

Sunday dinner was very quiet because there was only the family besides Aunt Lottie and Uncle Mart.

"What! No greasy dirty oil men?" exclaimed Aunt Lottie.

"Where's your boarders?" asked Uncle Mart.

"I had to tell 'em to go," said Mama sadly. "The house was so crowded with all the furniture and things we bought, I didn't have room for them."

"Why should you go on cooking for boarders?" demanded Lottie.

"I hated to see them go," said Mama. "They liked my cooking, and they didn't make a bit of trouble."

"Why should you cook for boarders," asked Aunt Lottie again, "now that you've come into all that money?"

"What money?" asked Grandpa, leaning back in his chair.

"*Your* money!" retorted Lottie. "Everybody says you're the richest man in the county."

Grandpa stuck his thumbs in the armholes of his vest, leaned back and beamed with pride. "They do, do they? Well, we got an idea we wanted to spend some of it . . ." He waved his hand. "Did you look things over, Lottie?"

They got up from the table and went into the front room.

"Della, I see you've got your piano," said Uncle Mart. "When will you start taking music lessons?"

"I'll play it for you," said Della. "It's a self-player. You pedal with your feet and the keys go up and down by themselves. I'll play *The Blue Danube*." She inserted a roll.

"Uncle Mart, I got me an Edison," said Bert. "I'll play it for you. I got an Atwater Kent radio too, but can't work it without electricity—forgot to get batteries." He put on a record.

The player-piano and the Edison began to make a lively clatter, playing different tunes. Orvie sat down beside Grandpa on the new overstuffed sofa that Papa had bought. Soon the music stopped. Bert put on another record and Della started the player-piano again.

"All you do is pedal!" she cried suddenly. "Canned music— that's no fun. I still want to take piano lessons and play it myself."

Bert threw the Edison record on the floor. "Sounds terrible. I don't like that one." He put on another, then began to beat his drum.

Addie came running into the room, crying. "Mama, I had six of my new dolls in one doll carriage," she wailed. "Shep got in the way and I bumped him and they all rolled down the back steps and every one broke."

"What do you care?" said Mama. "Oh Bert, do stop that noise."

"Never mind, Addie," said Della. "Grandpa will buy you a hundred more dolls tomorrow."

"Sure, Addie," said Grandpa. "As many as you want."

"Don't want any more dolls," screamed Addie. "I'm sick and tired of dolls."

"All right, Addie." Grandpa smiled. "Don't surprise me none."

Mama began to show Aunt Lottie her new purchases.

"Is this a whole new set of China?" gasped Aunt Lottie.

"Yes—one hundred pieces—Bird of Paradise pattern," said Mama. "Now I wish I'd taken Garden Bouquet instead."

"Remember that first set of dishes you got at Peg-Leg's store, long ago when you were first married?" asked Lottie. "The set with the gold band around?"

"I'm still using them," said Mama. "I fed the boarders on them. They're so thick, they don't break easy. This new set is so thin you can see through it. Somebody'd be sure to break a piece. I'll keep it locked up in this new china closet."

"And a new set of table silver!" exclaimed Lottie. "Solid or plated?"

"Solid," said Mama. "Remember that cheap set I got with coffee coupons? These are too good, and I won't have time to polish knives and forks every day."

"You're not going to use them?" asked Lottie.

"I should say not," said Mama. "And all these electric things— I can't use them either. We don't have electricity, so they're just clutterin' up the place. I don't know what I bought 'em for."

"You'll have to do what I told you," said Lottie. "Buy a house in town and move there."

"Oh!" exclaimed Della. "Wouldn't it be wonderful?"

"They're staking off new locations all over our quarter-section," said Papa. "There's to be one well on every ten-acre tract."

"Whew! Sixteen wells!" whistled Uncle Mart. "My! Ain't it nice to have rich relations!"

"They're goin' to use a new kind of rotary drill so they can go deeper," said Papa. "The new rigs will be of metal, not wood, and they'll be a lot higher and stronger. Most of the oil is in the deepest sand. The wooden rigs will soon be out of date."

"Sixteen wells, all on your farm! Ain't you glad?" cried Lottie.

"The Superintendent told me we will have to give up farming," Papa went on. "He advised us to move for our own safety. I always did say farming's a mighty slow way to make any money."

"You just better not leave this farm!" sputtered Bert.

"Oh, you'll like it in town," laughed Aunt Lottie. "You'll be close to the stores and everything!"

Bert marched angrily out the back door.

Mama shook her head. "That boy's still peddlin' milk and eggs to his customers. We don't need the money, and cows and chickens are a lot of trouble, but I can't make Bert stop."

"He'll stop soon enough," said Papa. "There'll soon be no place left for the cows. I'll have to sell off the stock."

"Since you've got to move," Grandpa spoke up, "why not try that house I showed you?"

"Who does it belong to?" asked Mama.

"To me!" said Grandpa. "While you was buyin' all them other things, I just up and bought us a house. It'll do you good to try it."

Mama told Aunt Lottie about the velvet carpets and lace curtains, and Della talked about the two bathrooms and hot and cold water. There would be electricity, so all the new appliances could be used. Before Aunt Lottie and Uncle Mart went away, the Robinson family had decided to move to town.

Orvie followed Grandpa out to his little house.

"Grandpa, did you buy that town house like you said?" he asked.

"Yes, Orvie," said Grandpa.

"Why do we have to go live there?"

"To learn a few things," said Grandpa, smiling.

"Are you coming with us?"

"No, Orvie, I'm comfortable here."

"I'll stay with you, Grandpa," said Orvie.

"Your Mama won't allow that," said Grandpa. "You'll have to go with the family."

"I don't know how I can leave Star and Shep . . ." said Orvie.

"I'll take good care of them for you," said Grandpa.

That evening a man came to the door and brought news for Papa and Grandpa. "The Tumbleweed Oil Company has staked a well and dug a cellar in the Prairie View cemetery," he said. "We've got to go over tonight."

Mama thought of her baby and of Mrs. Soaper's little girl. She thought of all the old families who had members buried there. "You won't let them drill, will you?"

"No," promised Papa and Grandpa. "We'll keep them out."

Mama saw the men put their six-shooters in their pockets. "You'll do it without fightin' and shootin', won't you?" she begged.

"Yes, if we can."

The men got in the car and rode away. Orvie had no desire to go with them, but he was ready to hear all about it when they came back next morning.

"What happened?" asked Mama.

"A picnic!" laughed Grandpa. "Half of our men stood guard, while the rest of us filled up the cellar hole. That's all we did—just shoveled the dirt back in."

"Was there any shootin'?" asked Orvie.

"Not a shot," said Grandpa. "We managed everything peaceable. The superintendent of the oil company got there at daylight. He was awful nice, admitted he was beat, and said he wouldn't bother the church people any more. Said he had not realized how strong the local people felt about it. He wasn't here thirty years ago, when we started that church for anybody who wanted to come, right after the Cherokee Run. We wanted a church to go to, and we couldn't see the harm of all going to the same one. We're still standin' together, the way we did then."

Later in the morning, the women and children from the box-car houses came to the Robinson well for water. They talked about the filling up of the cellar hole and the end of the church dispute. Orvie pumped up his bicycle tire and listened idly.

"I hear No. 5 Murray is soon comin' in," said Mrs. Decker.

"They got the torpedo hung in the well so late last night," said Mrs. Armstrong, "they decided to leave it there till this morning."

"What are you talking about—dynamite?" asked Mrs. Decker. "Wouldn't it be dangerous to leave it?"

"Why dangerous? Nothing can happen," Mrs. Armstrong went on. "Bill Barnes has been a shooter for twenty-two years, his wife told me."

"He'll do it once too often!" laughed Mrs. Decker. "Some day they'll pick him up in a coffee can."

Just then a car stopped in front of the house. Slim Rogers came in, and from the look on his face they all knew something terrible had happened. Della came running out, and Orvie hurried up to hear.

"I was there," said Slim, "over at No. 5 Murray. They sent a fellow to get a flashlight, and while he was gone, the superintendent of another company called to me. I went out to the road to his car, to talk to him. While we were talking, it happened. They brought the flashlight to the well, and they had the crowbar there, and . . . well . . . maybe they jolted it too much with the crowbar, nobody knows."

"Oh Slim!" Della broke into tears. "If you hadn't gone to talk to that man, it mighta been you too."

The other women looked stricken and white and said nothing. Orvie's lips were so dry he could not speak.

"Three men . . . wiped out in a minute," Slim managed to say. "Not a scratch or a bruise on 'em. Just snuffed out."

"Bill Barnes—Bill Barnes—was he hurt?" gasped Orvie.

"He's dead, Orvie," said Slim.

Orvie didn't wait. He ran as fast as he could over the plowed wheat field to Bonnie Jean's house. When he got there, the Osage Torpedo house was filled with people. There were so many men and women there, he hadn't the courage to crowd in. What could he say to Bonnie Jean anyway?

He walked slowly back home. He saw the wooden rigs rising up, gaunt frameworks against the sky on all sides of the Robinson farmhouse. Oil covered the slush-ponds and flowed into the wheatfields, where it was killing all green and growing things. Suddenly the boy hated oil—oil that had gotten into his blood and changed his life. Oil was a cruel monster, devouring people, striking them down. He saw his home and knew that he would soon have to leave it. Oil was taking it too.

Two days later, while making milk deliveries with Bert in the Ford, he rode past the Osage Torpedo house without stopping.

"The house is empty—they've moved away," he said.

Orvie knew he would never see Bonnie Jean again.

CHAPTER XIII

The New Home

"WELL, folks, how do you like it?"

It was Grandpa's hearty voice. The Robinsons all ran to the door to meet him. It was Sunday again, six months later, in the spring, but now they were living in the new house in town. Grandpa still lived in the little house under the cottonwood tree, and had driven to town in the old Ford.

"Why, Grandpa, you're all dressed up in new clothes!" cried Orvie.

It was true. Grandpa had on a new black and white check suit, a bright red necktie, shiny new shoes and a high wide Stetson hat. He took off his hat with a bow and tiptoed in on the velvet carpet.

"Why, Grandpa!" exclaimed all the others. "You're all dressed up!"

[164]

"Got to keep up with the rest of the family!" laughed the old man.

"How do you feel? Comfortable?" asked Mama.

"I'll choke to death if I can't soon take this tight collar off," growled Grandpa. "And my shoes are pinchin' my toes. But do I look like the richest man in the county?"

They all agreed that he did.

"Oh, Grandpa," cried Orvie. "How are Star and Shep? You takin' good care of 'em for me?"

"Sure, boy, sure," said Grandpa. "They're fine and dandy." He turned to the others. "Well, how do you like it here by this time?"

"Fine, Pa, fine," replied Papa.

"It's awful nice," said Mama. "Too nice for us."

"Are you using all the new things you bought, Jennie?" asked Grandpa. "Got the new wash-machine hooked up to the electricity?"

"Sure," laughed Mama. "I just sit on a chair now and wait for the washing to do itself."

Grandpa had stopped in before, but had never stayed long. Now Orvie and Addie showed him all over the house and explained everything. Addie turned the water on in the bathroom basin, so he could wash his hands, and Orvie explained how to take a shower.

"What! No tin wash-tub on Saturday night?" laughed Grandpa.

"Why, Grandpa," said Addie. "We live in the city now."

Mama roasted a chicken for dinner and served it on the Bird of Paradise china. The family ate it with the solid silver knives and forks.

[165]

"What's the matter with your cooking, Jennie?" asked Grandpa, pausing with a forkful of food half-way to his mouth. "It don't taste like it used to."

"It don't?" asked Mama. "Did I forget the salt?"

"Yes," said Grandpa. "Salt's been left out."

Della passed a shiny silver salt shaker, but Grandpa waved it away. "I don't mean that kind," he mumbled under his breath.

"The trouble about livin' in town," said Mama, when they went in the front room to sit down and visit, "there's nothing to do."

"Nothing to do?" asked Grandpa. Orvie came and sat on the sofa beside him.

"Can't listen to the player-piano all day long," said Della.

"Get sick of that old radio," growled Bert.

"No yard to play in, only the front sidewalk," said Addie.

"I never liked farming myself," Papa spoke up. "I never felt I was cut out for a farmer. But it was better to be doing something out in the air than sitting around in the house. Can't read the news-paper all day long!"

"There's just nothing to do," Mama went on. "No cows to milk, no chickens to feed, no eggs to gather, no boarders to cook for. I sure did hate to leave those cows . . ."

"What about all the racket of the oil wells?" demanded Grandpa.

"I got used to it," said Mama. "I haven't slept near so good since we came here. I miss the drilling."

"God bless my soul!" exclaimed Grandpa. "I never heard the like. You folks sure do beat all."

"The trouble is, Grandpa," said Orvie, "nothing ever *happens* in town. Why, on the farm a cow can get sick, or a horse can break a leg, or a storm will come up and you have to run to the storm cellar, or a cow gets lost and you have to ride the pony and hunt for her . . . the coyotes get in and kill some of the chickens . . . Nothing like that ever happens here in town." He paused. "Oh Grandpa, how's Shep? You been feedin' him good?"

"Sure," said Grandpa. "Whenever he comes around, I give him a bone."

"I like to died when I had to leave Star and Shep," said Orvie.

"I never thought I'd hate to leave that farm the way I did," said Mama.

"But you're close to the stores and everything," suggested Grandpa.

"I never want to see a store again," said Mama.

"Nor I," said Papa.

"Nor I," chimed in Della and Bert and Addie.

"Guess you cured us with that spending spree, Pa," said Mama. Grandpa chuckled. Orvie leaned over and squeezed his hand.

"But think of all the things you can *buy*!" persisted Grandpa.

"We're sick of buyin' things," said the family.

"But I thought you *wanted* to move to town!" snorted Grandpa. "You all said it would make you happy. You hated life on the farm with all those oil wells."

The whole family felt suddenly ashamed. They did not want to be ungrateful to Grandpa, who had done so much for them. Mama had been constantly reminding them of his generosity.

"You've been good to us, Pa," said Mama, "better than we deserve. But I guess we've all done a lot of thinking since we've moved to town. We've decided that money isn't everything."

"No?" Grandpa acted surprised. But Orvie knew he really

wasn't. Orvie squeezed his hand again.

"There's a big difference between buying with money you've earned and saved, and buying with money that's dropped into your lap," Mama went on. "A part of yourself goes into what you work and save for. That's why you get more pleasure out of it. Those knives and forks I got with coffee coupons . . . were more beautiful than solid silver to me."

"Remember that pink dotted swiss dress you sewed for me, Mama?" exclaimed Della. "You stayed up half the night to finish it, so I could speak my piece on Children's Day."

Mama laughed. "I bought it with my egg money," she said. "We didn't point to a dress in the show window then, and walk right in and buy it no matter what the price."

"Always wantin' things!" growled Bert. "Why can't folks be satisfied with what they got? Now on a farm, with horses and cows to take care of . . ."

"I never thought I'd miss those cows the way I do," said Mama. "Nobody likes to see their farm tore up the way ours was. If only oil hadn't come . . ."

"I'm not sorry we got the oil wells," said Grandpa. "The good Lord stored this wealth in the earth for his children, to see if they got the horse sense to use it right. As long as the oil field is there and bringin' in the money, we can't change that. Oil means progress."

"Progress!" sniffed Mama.

"I'll do the best I can with the money," Grandpa went on. "I'm pleased to be in on these big deals. Oil makes modern industry and transportation possible. I was readin' in a magazine about oil —they call it petroleum, and they make hundreds of things out of it—kerosene, gasoline, lubricants, asphalt, linoleum, varnish, paints, cold cream, perfume, vaseline and even hair tonic."

"They do?" laughed Mama. "What next?"

"We can't go backwards," Grandpa continued. "Oil has come and it hasn't spoiled *my* happiness none. Happiness just don't depend on a lot of money. Happiness is within yourself."

"What do you mean, Pa?" asked Mama.

"Just what I said," the old man repeated. "*Happiness don't depend on a lot of money.* Every one of you, except Orvie, thought it did, but you've learned by your own experience that it don't. I'm awful glad you've come to town and been so unhappy here."

"Pa! How can you say that?" cried Mama.

"You're glad we've been so unhappy here?" asked Della.

"Yes, that's why I bought this house," said Grandpa. "You wanted to live in town so bad, and I wanted you to find out for yourselves you wouldn't like it. My experiment worked. Just having a lot of money to spend hasn't made one of you happy, now has it?"

"No . . . no . . . no . . ." They were all ashamed, but they had to admit it.

"Town life don't agree with you folks, I can see that," said Grandpa. "Town life is like that chicken Jennie cooked today. Fine dishes and fine silver, but somethin' missin'—the salt left out." He paused.

"They talk about progress," he continued. "Why, there's never anything new. The same old things keep on givin' a man pleasure. To watch the green wheat grow and turn to gold at harvest time; to see trees blossom and bear fruit; to sweat good honest sweat doing hard work; to make friends of animals, wild and tame; to know the friendship of other men; to have time to think and hope, to work and pray—a man can't ask for more than that. *There are so many things that money cannot buy.* It can't buy happiness. I've been thinkin' about it ever since the first oil well came in . . ."

"Oh Pa!" Mama began to cry. "We've been so foolish. I guess all that money just turned our heads."

"How would you like to go back to the farm?" asked Grandpa quietly.

"Sure would!" cried Bert eagerly.

"Pa!" scolded Mama. "How can you tease us like this, when you know our farm's ruined?"

"Let's get in the Packard and go for a drive," suggested Grandpa.

They were soon out on the road, rolling through Bliss and Whizzbang, going south. It did not take long to come to the old Robinson place. They pulled up in front.

"Oh, I can't bear to look at it!" Mama hid her face in her hands.

The sight was indeed a sad one. There stood the old weather-beaten farmhouse in the midst of a sea of oil wells, machinery, smoke and steam. The front porch was sagging and great holes could be seen in the roof. The windows were broken and the old curtains, which Mama had not troubled to take down, were black with dirt and grease, and torn from blowing in the wind. Remnants of old broken-down furniture stood in the rooms and on the porch. Trees, shrubs and grass were dead. The yard was deep in dust where it was not a sea of seeping oil. The odor of oil and gas was overpowering.

The family looked and remembered how happy they had once been there. No one spoke, for they could not put their feelings into words.

[170]

Under the dead cottonwood tree on the left stood Grandpa's old brooder house, and not far from it Mama's old abandoned cook-stove.

"How can you stand it to go on living here, Pa?" asked Papa at last.

"Oh, I don't mind," laughed Grandpa. "I go fishing some days —off in the Indian Reservation, not around here. And I visit the oil men some. And I go to the store and visit some. I'm always happy no matter what happens."

"Do you get enough to eat?" asked Mama.

"Sure," laughed Grandpa. "That old cook-stove is wonderful— it gets plenty of draft settin' out in the wind. And I work pretty hard choppin' wood to burn. It helps me to pass the time."

"Oh, if only I had a wood stove again," sighed Mama. "They make the best biscuits in the world . . ."

"And I'd never complain about keepin' the woodbox full," said Orvie.

Grandpa looked at Mama. "Jennie, do you mean what you say?"

"Yes, cross my heart," said Mama. "Of course I know all that's over and somehow we got to get used to living in town . . ."

Grandpa told Papa to start the car up again, and they continued on down the road till they came to Cottonwood creek. Orvie called to Papa and they stopped.

The place was barely recognizable. There was no clear water down in the gully. There were no fish, no frogs—only red, greasy mud, saltwater and oil. The trees, bushes and vines that had once furnished comfortable shade were all dead or broken off to stumps. It was so desolate, even the campers had moved away, but they had left their litter behind.

Orvie thought of the happy days he had spent there. Nobody spoke, so Papa drove on, following Grandpa's directions. They all wondered where he was taking them. The ride was a long one, over country roads they had not been on before.

"My land, it's good to get out of an oil field," said Mama.

"Just look, they've got winter wheat planted," said Papa. "See how green it looks coming up."

"And the trees have green leaves on their branches," cried Addie, pointing.

"It's cooler here, with all the green things growing," said Della.

"I hear birds singing," said Orvie.

"Who are you takin' us to see?" asked Mama. "I don't know these folks. I never been here before."

The car stopped in front of a small farmhouse with a porch in front. The grass in the lawn was greening up from spring rains. There were a few flower beds and lilac bushes, and some trees. A small peach orchard grew near a vegetable garden. Barn, cowsheds and chicken coops could be seen at the back. There was a windmill and a storm-cellar.

The family stood and looked.

"It's as near like the old place as I could find," said Grandpa.

"Oh Pa, you don't mean it's for us?" cried Mama.

"It ain't got running water and two bathrooms," said Grandpa, "but there's a good well and a windmill. It ain't got gas or electricity, but that old cook-stove could be moved over easy . . ."

"We could get the kerosene lamps out of the old attic," said Della. "Maybe Slim and I can be married in the front room."

"So that's what's next!" laughed Grandpa. "Of course, since that original claim I took in the Cherokee Run has turned out so profitable, maybe after a while, we could afford a few improvements."

"Are you sure the oil companies won't come here and strike oil?" asked Papa.

"They've been and gone," said Grandpa. "Found nothing but dry holes, so we're safe."

"What about that expensive house in town?" asked Mama.

"I've already deeded it to Aunt Lottie and Uncle Mart," said Grandpa, "as a present from their rich relations! Town life suits them better than it does us. They'll be *near the stores and everything!*"

They all laughed.

"There's a whole quarter-section, Al," Grandpa went on. "Five acres in alfalfa, and the rest in wheat and pasture."

"Maybe I'm cut out for a farmer after all," laughed Papa.

"There's room for twenty or thirty cows in the barn," said Grandpa. "I've arranged to buy back all the stock you sold."

"Gosh!" exclaimed Bert. "I'll start a milk route."

[173]

"Sure, son," said Papa.

"There's a creek with lots of fish in it, Orvie."

"Golly, that's wonderful! Will you come and live with us, Grandpa?" asked Orvie, as they walked up on the porch of their new home. "And bring Star and Shep along with you?"

"You bet your boots I will!" laughed Grandpa. "I'll move my hen-house right over!"

*   *   *

Orvie and Bert made a number of trips back to the old farm with Grandpa to get the things that were needed. One day while Grandpa and Bert were loading the stove on the old wagon, Orvie ran out to No. 1 Robinson. The oil well was on a pump now, pumping oil out to two large tanks in the pasture. A big sign was nailed up, which said: Keep OUT This Means YOU. Orvie crawled under the barbed wire fence and started toward the derrick.

"Slim wouldn't care—there's no danger now," he said to himself.

He had picked up an old newspaper from the woodbox in the kitchen. He tucked it tightly under his arm and began to climb the ladder of the derrick.

"I always wanted to go to the top," he said softly. "I never did because Slim told me not to. I must do it, if I'm going to be a driller like Slim when I grow up."

Suddenly he knew that some day he would work in oil. He might be a driller like Slim, or he might do other important work, but it would be in oil. Oil had changed his life and gotten into

[174]

his blood. He knew the excitement and thrills it brought, he knew its hazards and tragedies. He knew its best and its worst, and it still held a fascination for him which he could not resist.

On and on, up and up the boy climbed. He stopped now and then to look down at the ground beneath him, but it did not make him dizzy. He reached the top and stepped out on the platform there.

It was a magnificent moment.

It was quiet and peaceful up there, except for the monotonous jogging of the pump below. The earth had flattened out, and the sky was a blue dome overhead. The sun was hot on Orvie's back and a good stiff wind was blowing. It was just the kind of day that he liked.

Orvie drew a deep breath. It was much higher than the old windmill in the pasture which he could see, a broken wreck in the distance. It was almost as good as being in the airplane again. He took the newspaper and began to tear off small pieces. He held the pieces out in the wind one at a time, and watched them blow away.

He watched each piece as it went. Where would they land—in the wheatfields of Kansas or the mountains of Arkansas or in far-away unknown places? The world was a wonderful place—a good place for many men to live and work, and to enjoy living and working. The world was a good place for a boy to live and grow to be a man.

The End

Words Defined

I

OIL TERMS

catwalk — a safety walk built around the outside of a rig.

crow's nest — the working platform at the top of the drill pipe, where the derrick man stands.

derrick or rig — the framework or tower over an oil well, for supporting the machinery used for boring, or for lifting or lowering it.

doghouse — the shed where the men change their clothes, or go for shelter.

dry hole or duster — a dry well, where no oil is found.

hijacking — the oil field term for robbery with firearms.

lazy bench — a bench in the engine house, under which the steam line originally passed.

nitro-glycerin — a colorless, heavy, oily explosive liquid.

spudding-in — the start of the actual drilling operation.

well, discovery — the first well that produces oil in a new district.

well, offset — a well directly opposite on adjoining property.

well, wildcat — the first well drilled in a new district.

Other oil terms or expressions used have been defined in the text.

II

GENERAL TERMS

claim — an area of land claimed by a settler and marked by staking. Each settler who made the Cherokee Run picked out a quarter-section of land for his "claim" and staked it off, to keep other settlers away. He had to "file his claim" at the land-office.

eighty — implies 80 acres, one half of a quarter-section. "South eighty" means the south half of a 160 acre farm.

hames, housing — parts of the harness of a team of horses.

Osages, Otoes — two of the many tribes of Oklahoma Indians.

section — a square mile of land, containing 640 acres. Quarter-section: one-fourth of a square mile of land or 160 acres. Oklahoma was surveyed in sections, with straight roads running east and west, and north and south, at one mile intersections. The size of each settler's claim was one-quarter section, or 160 acres. This meant there were only four settlers (families) to each square mile.

sod-house — a cave built of layers of prairie sod grass, usually on a slope, with dirt walls and floor, by the first white settlers in Oklahoma (and other western states).

Sooner — originally a term of contempt for a "claim-jumper"—a person who settled on government land before it was legally open to settlement.

Stetson hat — western cowboy style hat of pale cream-colored felt, with high crown and wide brim.

still — an apparatus for distilling liquor.

tow sack — a burlap bag; in some parts of the country called a croker sack.

W.C.T.U.—Women's Christian Temperance Union. Although "no saloons" was a part of the Oklahoma Constitution written in 1907, this organization has always been active in the state, in an endless war against "bootleggers."